Accidental Baby for the Billionaire

An Enemies to Lovers Second Chance Romance

Josie Hart

Contents

Prologue – Ava

"Another!" I said, leaning on the bar. My heels were killing me, and standing on them had become hard now that the world was spinning slowly around me. Everything seemed to have tilted on its axis.

"Are you sure you should drink more?" the bartender asked.

"Come on...Johnny." I squinted to read the name tag on the bartender's shirt. "Are you cutting me off?"

"Are you driving?" he asked.

"No way," I said and giggled. "I'm way too drunk for that."

He grinned and raised his eyebrows at me.

"I came in a cab, Johnny. Come on, just one more. My dad died this week, and I can't face the real shit sober."

At that confession, Johnny's face fell.

"I'm sorry," he said and grabbed a glass to pour me another vodka cranberry.

"That's a great line," someone said next to me.

When I looked up at him, the bluest eyes I'd ever seen looked down at me. And God, this man was *hot*. At least, I was pretty sure he was hot…I was really drunk. But he looked edible. Bronze skin, sandy hair, and those eyes—the color the sky was named after.

"I'll have to remember it for when Johnny over here wants to cut me off next," he added.

I shook my head. "It's not a line. My dad died this week. See the black dress? We buried him today."

The handsome stranger glanced down at me, and back up at my face. Maybe my expression told him how dead serious I was.

"Shit," he breathed. "I'm sorry."

"Yeah," I said. I wrapped my fingers around the full glass Johnny pushed in front of me. "Me too."

"What happened?"

"Does it matter?" I asked. "He's gone." And he left us with a mountain of debt my mom and I hadn't known about. How the fuck did someone do that to their family? How had he hidden it from us for so long that he'd gambled and drank all the money away? Now, the banks were after us for the money. They didn't care that it wasn't our fault. They didn't care that we didn't have the money to fix it. By definition, the fact that they were coming after us for it meant that it was *our* money that he'd gambled away.

I shook it off.

"Enough about me," I said with a smile. "Tell me about you. You're way too attractive to hang out in a joint like this."

He laughed, surprised. "Are you using a line on me?"

"Did it sound like a line?" I asked and sucked on the straw in my glass. I was being ridiculously flirtatious.

"It sounded like the kind of line I would have used on a girl like you," he said.

I giggled again. "Well, now that the line is out of the way...I'm Ava."

"Ava...do you have a last name?"

"You bet," I said. "And I'm not giving it to you."

"What?" He looked confused.

"There are way too many stalkers out there, you know? And God knows what people can do with next to no information at all these days."

"You think I'm a stalker?" he asked, his face a mixture of a frown and a grin.

I tilted my head to study him. The room swam around me, but his angelic face was in perfect focus.

I shook my head.

"No, you're right. Stalkers are usually less attractive."

He burst out laughing. "It sounds like you have experience. I'm Noah."

"Noah. Well, if my ex is anything to go by...I mean, you know how people say it's not about looks, it's about personality? It's such a noble thing to say. But it turns out he wasn't hot *or* interesting."

Noah kept laughing. "I would hate to get on your bad side."

I sighed. "Yeah, you wouldn't want that."

"So, how about I get on your good side?" he asked. He took a small step closer to me. His cologne wrapped around me, and I breathed in deeply. I was drunk. And that made me horny. And this man was like a gift from the gods on a night like tonight, when it felt like my whole world had fallen apart.

"How are you going to do that?" I asked.

He kissed me. I melted against him, and he wrapped an arm around my waist, cupping my cheek with his other hand. His tongue slid into my mouth, and he tasted just as good as I figured he would.

When he broke the kiss, my skin was hot.

"Like that," he said. "Did it work?"

I nodded and swallowed hard. "Yeah, it worked."

He smiled at me again, a charming smile that made me weak in the knees.

"How about we get out of here?" I asked. "I happen to have more good sides you can get on."

"Yeah?" He grinned, already taking out his wallet to pay for our drinks.

I didn't usually do this. I wasn't the type to initiate a one-night stand or sleep with strangers. But I'd broken up with Kyle two weeks ago, and a week later, my dad had died of a heart attack. And just like that, everything about my life changed.

I just wanted to do something that wasn't *me*. I wanted to do something that made me feel like this wasn't *my* life.

"Let's get out of here," he said and took my hand.

I let him lead me out of the bar. A black car pulled up a moment later. I frowned.

"Is this a cab?"

"No," he chuckled. "I sent for my car."

"You have a car you send for?"

He grinned at me, again looking a little baffled.

"You don't have any idea who I am, do you?"

"Should I?" I asked.

He shook his head. "No, you shouldn't. But in a short while, I'll show you exactly who I am."

I giggled again, and he opened the car door for me, letting me get in first.

"Where do you live?" he asked.

I hesitated.

"I'm not going to stalk you," he added.

I laughed, feeling stupid, and gave the driver my address. Noah was on me in a flash, his lips on my neck, nibbling the delicate skin. His hand cupped my breast, massaging and kneading. We were way past baby steps and taking it slow. But I'd asked for this when I'd told him to come home with me.

We were going to do this. I needed him to fuck my brains out so that I would stop thinking about the hell my life had become. I needed him to worship my body, to make me feel so good that nothing else mattered anymore.

When Noah slid his hand down my crotch, it was a silent promise that he would deliver.

The house was dark when we got out of the car.

"You live here?" he asked, looking at the old house. It was a large house with a gabled roof, half-timbering, and a covered porch, straight from the Victorian era.

"Well, I do now," I said. "My mom needed help after...so I moved back home."

"She's not here, is she?" Noah asked, his steps faltering.

"God, no. I wouldn't invite you back if she were. She's out tonight. She'll be back tomorrow."

Noah let out a breath and ran his hand through his hair.

"Not a fan of meeting the parents, huh?" I asked.

Noah shook his head. "That's not how I play the game."

We climbed the steps onto the porch, and I turned to him, running my hands over his chiseled chest. "A game, huh?"

"You bet this is a game," he said, nibbling my lower lip, and talking through his kisses.

"Well, a game should have rules," I said in a breathy voice. God, I wanted him so badly.

"Okay, rule number one...no clothes."

I giggled and pushed the front door open.

Noah started undressing me the moment the door was shut, and we were alone inside. He pulled my dress over my head and dropped kisses along my shoulder while he unclasped my bra.

I fiddled with the buttons on his shirt and peeled it off his shoulders. He was built like a *god*. The muscles moved under his skin as he pulled off my bra and ran his hands down my back.

When he pushed me against the living room wall, I gasped from the cold. But Noah's mouth found a nipple, and I forgot all about the temperature in the room.

I gasped as he sucked on my nipples—first, the right one, and then the left. I groaned when he massaged and squeezed my breasts, pushing them together and planting kisses between them.

I fiddled with his buckle while he kissed, nibbled, licked, and sucked me. When I undid his button and zipper, I reached into his pants and pulled his cock free.

He was impressive, with silky smooth skin, and the tip was slick with lust.

I ran my thumb over the tip of his cock, and Noah groaned.

"You're driving me crazy," he said.

"I know," I murmured and pulled away from his grasp and onto my knees.

Noah groaned and pushed his hips forward. I sucked the tip of his cock into my mouth and swirled my tongue around it, tasting the saltiness of his need for me. When I sank my head further into him, taking him deeper and deeper into my mouth, Noah sucked a breath through his teeth. He pushed his fingers into my dark hair, curling them into fists, and pulled me closer. He pushed further and further down my throat.

I bobbed my head back and forth, stroking him in and out of my mouth. I got wetter and wetter as I sucked him off, melting into my panties.

"Fuck, Ava," Noah said through gritted teeth, and he yanked back so that his cock slipped from my mouth with a plop. "I'm going to lose it, and I want to be inside of you when I do."

He grabbed my hand and pulled me up, kissing me hard before I could reply.

"Where's your room?" he mumbled.

I took his hand and teetered half-naked on my heels toward my bedroom. When we stepped into the room, Noah pulled my panties down from behind, and I kicked off my shoes. He grabbed my ass with one hand and cupped my pussy around the front with the other. He ground his cock against my ass, and I moaned.

When he ran his hand up my back, he pushed me forward, so that I leaned on my bed, naked and ready for him.

Noah ran his hand between my legs, his fingers finding my slit.

"You're so wet," he said.

"Yeah," I answered simply.

None of this was like me. But it felt so good to just live in the moment.

Noah paused, retrieving his hand. His pants rustled as he kicked them off. I heard the rip of a foil packet. When he touched me again, he gripped my hips, and the rubbery tip of his condom-wrapped cock pressed against my entrance. I gasped, and Noah pushed into me. He moved slowly like he was as aware of his size as I was. I moaned as he slid into me, filling me up.

When he was buried to the hilt, his hips flush against my ass, I paused, trembling around him.

He pulled back and pushed into me again, and I cried out as he started to fuck me. Noah picked up his pace, stroking in and out of me, and I moaned and cried out as he pounded into me harder and harder. His balls slapped against my pussy, and every stroke was pure pleasure.

In no time, an orgasm built inside me, his cock stroking me in all the right places so that the pleasure burned and grew inside me.

When I orgasmed, my pussy clamped down around Noah's cock, and he gritted his teeth and grunted. He gripped my hips, fingers digging into my skin, and I sank my chest onto the mattress, weakened with the pleasure that crashed into me with every stroke.

I trembled, and Noah bent over me, planting a kiss on my back.

When he pulled out, I moaned again.

I rolled over and shifted onto the mattress. Noah crawled over me, and my legs fell open for him. He positioned himself between my legs and slid into me again.

He kissed me, and his eyes locked on mine when he bucked his hips again, fucking me anew. He rammed into me harder and harder, breathing hard. His lips were fractions away from mine, our gasps and moans mingling and twisting together, and I held onto his shoulders as he rode me.

My second orgasm wasn't far off—alcohol always loosened me up. I came that much easier in this state.

When I cried out, grabbing onto Noah's shoulders and holding on as the orgasm ripped through me a second time, Noah bit out a cry.

He was right there with me.

His cock jerked and pulsed inside me as my body contracted, milking him as we came together.

When it was over, Noah collapsed on top of me, out of breath.

He rolled off a second later, allowing me to breathe.

"Fuck," he said in a breathy voice. "That was fucking incredible."

"It was," I said with a smile.

"You were right. You had plenty more good sides to you."

I giggled and pressed my hand against my forehead. The alcohol was starting to wear off, and now that I'd had a release to take care of the urgent need that had ruled me the last couple of days, reality started to set in.

Noah was a stranger. And I'd brought him back to my place.

I sat up and crossed my arms over my chest.

"You should probably go," I said softly.

Noah sat up, too. He frowned. "Why?"

"Because I don't usually do this. I'm a mess right now. I have a lot of stuff to work through. I mean, this was great, but—"

"Hey, it's okay," Noah said gently. "I get it."

"You do?"

He nodded. "I know all about what it's like to try to get away from the life you usually live."

I let out a shuddering breath. "Thank you."

"It's going to be okay in the end," he said. "And if it's not okay, it's not the end."

I rolled my eyes and snorted. "You know that line is all over the internet, right?"

He shrugged. "It's still true."

"Hmm," I said.

"Can I call you?" he asked.

I frowned. "Why?"

"Because I don't want to be the guy who hit and run when you're going through hell."

I giggled despite the unsettled feeling in my stomach. "That's what you call it?"

He shrugged. "I prefer to cuddle after sex, but I know you need your space. So, compromise."

I nodded. "Yeah, okay."

He shifted off my bed to find his phone in his pants that he'd kicked off and handed it to me. I programmed my number into it.

"Ava," he said with a grin.

"No last name."

He laughed and pulled on his pants. I found an oversized shirt and a pair of shorts in my closet and pulled them on to let him out.

"I'll call you," he said when we walked to the front door together.

"Will you?" I asked.

He nodded. "Of course." He flashed another of his charming grins at me before he turned.

The black car that had brought us appeared out of nowhere, and Noah climbed in. When the car drove off, I closed the door and leaned against it.

My body felt amazing after having had sex. And alcohol. But neither of those had driven away the fact that my dad was dead and he'd left us with a shit ton of debt.

But I will figure that out again tomorrow. Right now, I needed headache tablets, water, and sleep.

1

Ava

One Year Later

"I'm home," I called out, hanging my keys on the hook behind the door. I put down my handbag and kicked off my heels, curling my toes downward. My feet ached after a full day on them.

I arched my back, hearing my spine pop. This was the fifth day in a row I'd worked overtime, and I was exhausted.

My mom didn't answer me.

I picked up the stack of mail next to my handbag and sifted through them. They were all for my mom, but they were all bills. I knew the envelopes by now. Looking at the stack of bills made my stomach twist. There was no way I would get all those taken care of on my measly salary. Not where I was now.

"Mom?" I called again. I fished a red envelope from the center of the stack and tore it open.

It was a final notice of foreclosure on the house.

I squeezed my eyes shut. I'd known this was coming, but now that it was here, I felt sick to my stomach.

It meant we only had thirty days to pay the outstanding mortgage, or we were out on the street. And I had no idea how we could get that money together in a month.

"Mom?" I asked, again, padding on stockinged feet through the house. The setting sun fell into the windows, casting lines of gold on the floor.

When I popped my head into my mom's room, she was asleep on her bed. She looked thin and frail—a shell of the woman she used to be.

I tiptoed into the room and pulled a blanket over her. She sighed, her brow furrowed in worry even as she slept.

"We'll figure it out," I whispered, and stroked my fingers through her hair once before I left her room again.

I hoped to God we could figure it out. Mom hadn't worked since Dad had died. The grief had sent her spiraling into depression, and instead of giving her the time she needed to recover, they'd let her go. Finding out about all the debt my dad had left behind for us had only made it worse.

I'd moved back in to take care of her, to help her pay the bills. I couldn't just leave her.

After a year, I couldn't do what I'd set out to do—I couldn't save her or the house.

My phone beeped with a message from Paige.

Are we still on for tonight?

Before I could type an answer, my phone rang. I didn't recognize the number.

"Am I speaking to Ava Brooks?" a female voice asked on the other side of the line.

"Speaking," I said. If this was another debt collector trying to track us down, I would throw my phone against a wall.

"This is Belinda Byers. I'm calling you from Solomon, Forger, and Riggs."

My stomach twisted again, this time with hope.

"Oh, I've been waiting for your call." I'd given up hope, thinking that the call wouldn't come. And they wouldn't call me if I didn't make it through, right? That was what they always said after interviews and applications—if I didn't hear back from them in two weeks, I had to assume it was unsuccessful. She wouldn't call me to tell me I'd failed.

Again.

"I'm happy to say that your application was successful. The managing partners have reviewed your resume and considered your interview recording. We'd like to invite you to work for us."

"Oh," I breathed. "Yes. Thank you."

"We'll see you on Monday, Miss Brooks."

"I'll be there," I said.

I remained composed until we ended the call. As soon as I ended the call and I was sure Belinda Byers wouldn't hear me, I squealed and threw my hands up in the air.

Finally! I was catching a break.

This was the third law firm I'd applied to, in the hopes that I could land a better job with a higher salary. I needed the financial boost. I needed something—anything—that would get us by.

I considered waking my mom to let her know, but decided against it. The poor woman barely slept at night. She was stressed and depressed. I wanted her to get all the sleep she could get.

Instead, I picked up my phone and typed a reply to Paige.

We're on. I'll meet you at nine.

I hopped into the shower and washed off the day, changed into jeans and a top and ballerina flats—no heels for me—and pulled my hair back into a ponytail.

Before I left, I took a microwave meal from the freezer and prepared it for when my mom woke up. I left it on the counter with a note.

I got the job! Have dinner, I'm out with Paige. I love you!

I left the house quietly and drove into town.

The Seattle skyline was breathtaking at night. The space needle, along with all the tall buildings, created an urban backdrop against the inky sky, and as the sun sank away further and further, the lights in the city came on. Up above, stars were pinpricks of light in the sky, as if the heavens reflected the city below.

I walked into Olive and Twist and glanced around. Paige waved at me from a booth.

"Did you only get off work now?" she asked when I hugged her.

"Not too long ago. I had time to shower and change. You'll notice I'm not meeting you in a pencil skirt and heels."

"It's a nice change," Paige said, rolling her eyes before she grinned at me. "You work too hard."

"Someone has to do it," I said.

When we sat down, Paige pushed an Apple Martini in my direction.

"You're a saint," I said and lifted the glass to my lips to take a sip. "I have news."

"Yeah?" Her green eyes sparkled.

"We're losing the house."

Paige frowned. "I thought you had good news."

I nodded. "I do. I got the job with Solomon, Forger, and Riggs."

"What!?" Paige cried out. "Ava, that's amazing! You should have led with that. What the hell!"

I giggled, and when Paige lifted her glass in salute, I clinked mine against hers. We each took a sip.

"It's a big increase, and I start on Monday," I said. "But that doesn't mean we'll definitely keep the house. We still have so much to take care of, and they're after me like I'm the one that fucked up. Debt collectors are a special brand of evil."

Paige shook her head and glanced across the bar.

"It's ridiculous that they're willing to put you out of your house after what your dad did. And with your mom in her condition..."

"I know," I said. "But there's no use feeling sorry about it now. It is what it is. I just have to figure something out."

"Will you be working with Noah Forger?" Paige asked.

"Who?"

The look she gave me made me burst into giggles.

"He's only the god of the legal world," Paige said.

"I know, I know. I was kidding," I said. "I know who he is. I've heard the name. And I'll be an idiot if I don't know my new boss's son's name. Although I heard he believes he is god's gift to mankind, that he's doing everyone a favor just by being on this earth."

"You forget to mention how drop-dead *gorgeous* he is," Paige pointed out.

"I don't actually know what he looks like," I admitted.

Page shook her head. "Well, he's *dreamy*. That counts for something. And he's a top-shelf lawyer. I'm jealous you get to look at that face all day every day come Monday."

I laughed and shook my head. "I don't know if I'll be working with him. He might be on a different floor. I doubt he'll notice a measly paralegal like me anyway."

"Don't you dare talk about yourself that way."

"That's how he'll see me," I said with a shrug. "Besides, I don't care about him. I care about his dad, Archibald Forger, and the fact that he's signing my paychecks. It's all about who you keep happy."

"You've always been so diplomatic," Paige said with a grin. "What will you do if you end up losing the house?"

I shivered just thinking about it. But it was a very real possibility.

"We'll figure it out. I think I can afford something small for the two of us, just to get us back on our feet. I can sell whatever won't fit in a new apartment, and we'll take it from there."

Paige shook her head and ran her fingers through her light brown hair.

"I wish I could help somehow. If I had the cash, I'd bail you out in a snap."

"I know," I said.

Paige was a personal assistant to the CEO of a company in town. I kept forgetting what it was the company actually did. I just knew that Paige practically ran the guy's whole life. She was the kind of person who had everything under control. She could multitask like a demon and look good while doing it.

"You probably wouldn't have accepted it anyway," Paige said with a laugh. "You never accept help, not even from Kyle when you two were together."

I snorted. "Like Kyle ever had something to offer that would help. Seriously, he had his hands full saving his own ship from sinking, let alone mine."

Paige laughed.

"He called me two days ago," I said.

"What?" Paige cried out. "Really?"

I nodded and swirled my drink. "Yeah, he said he wanted to meet up, that he feels like we have unfinished business."

"Are you going to meet him?"

"God, no," I said and rolled my eyes. "I can tell you what his 'unfinished business' is. That new girl of his probably dumped him, and he's fresh out of options for a wife. You know he just wants to get married. He doesn't care to who. So, he's going back to the drawing board. But I have enough problems as it is."

"I think you're better off without him, anyway." Paige leaned on the bar and tilted her head so that her blonde hair hung over her shoulder.

"I thought you disapproved of me being single."

"I'd rather you're single than with *him*," Paige said.

I laughed and nodded.

"It's a pity that guy never called you back," she added.

"What guy?"

"The one you slept with."

I groaned. "That was a year ago, and I wasn't looking for anything serious. It was just a one-night stand. And so unlike me, anyway."

That was true, but it pissed me off that he hadn't called me back after he'd told me he would. I hadn't asked for it, he'd offered. But whatever, it didn't matter.

It was a hit and run, just like he'd said.

I shook my head and forced myself to get back to the topic. "Thanks for being so caring, Paige. But you don't have to even *think* about helping me. This isn't your mess to deal with."

Paige sipped her martini. "It's not your mess, either," she pointed out.

I nodded. She was right—this mess was all my dad's. It was convenient for him that he'd checked out early, leaving the bullshit for my mom to deal with. I missed him—a lot. Sometimes I wished I could go back in time. Not only to see him again, but to shake him by the shoulders and ask him what the hell he was thinking.

How could he have done that to my mom? To me?

He must have known that something like this could happen. Like I kept telling Paige, there was no use looking back at the past and wondering how things might have been different. I had to deal with what was in front of me.

Maybe one day, far into the future, we will finally be rid of this burden. My mom would be okay again, and I would be able to live my life.

"My house is always open for you. You know that, right?"

I nodded. Paige was a great friend. No matter what, she would help where she could. We'd been friends since grade school, and she'd had my back since day one when we'd decided to be best friends forever.

No matter how badly things went, though, I wasn't going to impose on her space. Paige lived in a loft apartment, and I wasn't going to barge in on her privacy with my mom and all of our stuff.

"So, what are you doing about the bar exam?" Paige asked, changing topics on me. "They're going to let you work there as a lawyer once you pass, right?"

"I'm not taking the exam again," I said.

"Come on, why not?" Paige asked.

"Because after failing it twice, I get the message loud and clear." I sighed heavily and drained my martini glass. "I'm just not meant to be a lawyer."

"That's bullshit. I've never seen anyone on their toes like you. You can argue with anyone into a corner, with a memory like an elephant, and you miss nothing. They'll be lucky to have you. You just have to pass that exam. Third time's a charm."

I laughed and lifted my hand to flag a server so we could order another round.

"Are you hungry?" I asked. "I haven't eaten yet."

"Sure, let's split it."

I nodded.

"You're not going to distract me from the topic with food," Paige warned.

I chuckled. "Wouldn't dream of pulling one over on you."

The server appeared, and we ordered more martinis and a platter of food to share. As soon as the server left with our order, Paige got on with me about passing the bar exam and finally becoming a lawyer like I'd always dreamed of. But that wasn't going to happen any time soon.

I sucked at writing exams. I clammed up, getting some kind of stage fright, and everything I'd studied flew out of my head as if I'd never studied anything at all.

It looked like being a paralegal was my future.

And right now, all I cared about was paying the bills so Mom and I could finally breathe again. I would focus on fulfilling my dreams again another time.

2

Noah

As soon as the elevator doors slid shut, she shimmied her scantily clad body against mine.

"Noah," she murmured.

"Don't," I said, stepping away. "There are cameras in here."

She came closer again and nibbled the skin on my neck.

"I don't care. I doubt it's anything the security team hasn't seen before."

I pushed her away again.

"I'm serious."

She pouted. "But you're Noah Forger. What are they going to do, put you out of the building? You *own* the building."

She wasn't wrong, but I wasn't going to make a public spectacle of myself. Sure, I was Seattle's playboy, the guy who got all the ass. Women wanted me for my looks, for my money, to be associated with me so that they could brag to their friends and earn some clout in their social circles.

But I wasn't going to throw away my business reputation just like that. It was common knowledge I slept around, but far be it from me to give anyone the ammo to shoot me down. A photoshoot in the elevator with a woman whose name I barely remembered wasn't how I planned to go down in history.

I was a Forger, after all. The name meant something.

"Let's just wait until we get to my apartment," I muttered.

She sighed and nodded, stepping back. She was a pain in the ass, but I wanted someone to fuck tonight, so I'd deal with her. She complained about everything, but I could think of a couple of ways to keep her mouth occupied.

Not that any of them really *satisfied* me. Whenever I slept with someone it took the edge off, and helped me down from the ledge when I was wired as fuck. But it always left me empty.

The alternative was abstinence, though. And what the fuck was that going to help?

We waited until the elevator doors pinged, and opened into my personal lobby. I pushed open the front door and pulled her in.

As soon as we were inside, she was on me again. This time, I didn't fight her. She pushed her hands into my hair and muttered something unintelligible.

Someone cleared a throat behind me, and I froze.

The woman yelped and jumped away from me, covering her arms over her chest as if she was naked already. Aside from ruffled hair and a whole lot of lust going around, there wasn't much to see.

When I turned, my dad sat on a leather armchair in my living room, looking bored. He'd loosened his tie and rolled his sleeves up halfway, but that was about as casual as he would ever get. He always looked like he'd just stepped out of the office.

Even when it was past midnight.

I groaned. "Seriously, Dad?"

"That's your dad?" she asked.

"What are you doing here?" I asked, ignoring her.

He looked pointedly at the woman. I rolled my eyes and turned to her.

"Sorry, babe. I'll have to catch up with you next time."

"You're kicking *me* out?" she cried out.

I pushed my hands into my pockets.

"It's Archibald Forger." I shrugged in a whatcha-gonna-do way.

She glared at me. "Fine."

I opened the door for her, and she stormed toward the elevator, not looking back. I closed the door and leaned against it.

"Way to kill the mood," I said to my dad. "What do you want?"

"Don't take that tone with me, Noah. Jesus, are you going to fuck the whole of Seattle?"

I shrugged. "If they're offering. Do you want a drink?" I walked to the wet bar on the far side of the room.

"No. Are you drunk?"

"Not drunker than usual," I said and poured myself three fingers of whiskey in a tumbler. These days, it took a hell of a lot of alcohol just to get me on the right level.

"You shouldn't be drinking," Dad said.

I looked him in the eye and threw back the alcohol.

He scowled. "You're thirty, Noah—"

"I was going to check my ID to be sure, but now that you've reminded me, I don't have to."

"Stop your shit. God, I'm so over your attitude. You can't act like a damn teenager, drinking your way through all the bars in Seattle, and fucking anything with a pair of tits."

I grinned. I wanted to tell him that he'd be upset if it *didn't* have a pair of tits, but that would be pushing it. My dad could be scary as hell when he was angry, and I knew just how hard I could push.

I poured another drink before sitting down on the closest couch armrest.

"What's the problem, Dad? I'm not doing anything wrong. I'm allowed to drink and have fun. Hell, I even keep it out of the papers and off the screens. That's something, right? I work hard, I win all my cases, and I single-handedly brought in most of the clients we got this year."

"Yeah, and you pissed away your bonuses the moment they landed in your account. Don't get me started on your gambling."

"Don't tell me what to do with my money," I snapped.

He could be a dick about a lot of things, telling me how to live my life, but I earned my money, and if I wanted to spend it, that was my prerogative. No matter where, no matter how.

"You're a disgrace," Dad growled. I bristled at that.

"Just because I'm not buttoned up to the throat, and serious as fuck with a stick up my ass doesn't mean I'm not worthy of the Forger name."

"Carry on like this, and I'll have to make it public that you're not," Dad said.

"So, what, you'll disown me?"

Dad shook his head. "I won't disown you. I'm not like that."

I snorted. "How reassuring."

"But you can bet your ass you're not going to make partner if you keep going like this."

"What!?" All I've wanted since the day I joined my father's law firm was to make partner. I was a fucking Forger—my name was up on the wall, too. Even though my dad was managing partner now, that would change one day. But I had to climb the ranks first. I was already one of the youngest senior associates in the firm. Making partner so soon would be a feat.

Unless my dad was full of shit.

"You heard me," Dad said. "I'm not letting you become a partner in my law firm if you can't behave yourself. We have a name, a reputation to uphold, and you're ruining it by acting like this whole thing is a game. I'm already under scrutiny because you being in the firm at all is a matter of nepotism."

"I'm at the firm because I'm fucking good at my job," I said hotly. "It's got nothing to do with the fact that I'm your son."

"The fact that you're my son is the reason you're still where you are. Anyone else would have been demoted or fired for acting the way you do."

"No one can fire me for being a great lawyer. That's what's keeping me there. I earn my place in the firm fair and square, and you're not going to tell me anything else. They can call it nepotism if they want, but who gives a shit what they think, anyway?"

"I do," Dad said. He pushed his hands into his pockets. "And since public opinion and word of mouth is how we get most of our clients, you better give a shit about that, too."

I shook my head and drained my second glass of whiskey. I was aching for a third, but if my dad had an issue with how I did things, drinking more alcohol wouldn't help my situation.

"So, what, stop drinking and stop fucking around? Is that what you want?"

"I want you to grow up," Dad said, walking to the door.

"Where are you going?" I asked.

"Home."

When he shut the door behind him, I groaned and lifted the glass into the air, ready to smash it against a wall. Instead, I lowered it and put it on the bar.

I walked to the bedroom and stripped off my clothes. Looked like I was going to bed alone tonight.

———ele———

"I can't believe he cock-blocked you," Gunner laughed.

I shook my head. "We weren't that far, yet. But she thought I had to get rid of him, not the other way around."

"Holy shit," Aaron bellowed and laughed. "I can't believe it. Does she even know who Archibald Forger is?"

"She knew who I was, and that was all I cared about," I said grimly. "But whatever. That ship has sailed. I doubt I'll see her again, and good riddance, too. But my dad wants me to really straighten my shit out, and I don't want to do that. Not the way he wants, anyway."

I sat with Gunner and Aaron on the brown leather Chesterfield couches that graced the large living room area at the Cavaliers' headquarters. It was just a posh bar, with exclusive membership. But as far back as anyone could remember, the men who attended Maple Park Academy, and then Westside University, all joined the Cavaliers, a men's club where we drank expensive alcohol and smoked cigars and bragged about how great we were. It sounded elitist.

And I guess it was.

But it was tradition, and the most important thing to the upper crust of the exclusive Seattle society was tradition and legacy.

"Maybe he has a point," Gunner said.

I frowned at him. "Tell me you didn't just agree with that old bastard that I'm screwing up."

"You have a legacy to protect, you know," Gunner said. "We all do."

"Yeah," Aaron said. "I mean, can you imagine what my dad would say if I acted like that? I'd lose the bank."

I rolled my eyes. "You can't lose something you own just by having fun, you know. And you..." I glared at Gunner. "You're the CFO of your dad's company."

"And I got there by walking the straight and narrow, my friend," Gunner said.

I shook my head. "Pussies, the both of you. I just want to enjoy myself. What's the point of being a Forger, of having all this money I work so damn hard for, if I can't do anything with it?"

Gunner burst out laughing. "You didn't work hard for your money. You were born with one of the biggest trust funds out there."

I shrugged. "Yeah, well, I do earn my own money too, you know."

Gunner nodded and took a sip of his drink. He'd been sitting with the same glass of whiskey for almost three hours. And Aaron wasn't even drinking anything. My head throbbed after last night. I drank beer just to take the edge off. Bite the dog that bit you. Isn't that how the saying goes?

"What does your dad want you to do, exactly?" Aaron asked.

"Just stop fucking around," I said.

"Is that all? Not stop drinking, date someone, or something?"

"God, no," I said. "And thank fuck for that. Can you imagine me with a girlfriend?" I snorted.

Gunner and Aaron glanced at each other.

"If either of you even mentions Adele..."

"Hey, you were the one who said it," Aaron said, holding up his hands. "We weren't going to mention the fact that you had the perfect girl."

I nodded. "Yeah, until she fucked someone else."

Gunner punched Aaron in the arm.

"What was that for?" Aaron asked.

"Being a dick," Gunner said. "Seriously, you walked a similar path, and we don't rub your nose in it."

Aaron's face clouded over. We'd all had shit relationships in the past. I'd been lucky—I'd figured out who Adele was before I'd married her. And she'd taught me to put myself first, anyway. The safest way to prevent what she'd done to me from happening again was to hit and run, to fuck and forget, to play the game the right way. The terms were simple. I didn't do love, and I always wore a condom.

It was the easiest way not to get into shit of the permanent variety.

"Maybe you should just think about what your dad is asking of you," Aaron finally said.

"I'll just lie low until he gets over his mood," I said. "He'll get busy with some project, and then I can do what I want again. He's just bored right now."

I glanced toward the bar where my dad stood with Zeke Solomon and Maurice Riggs. No doubt, the managing partners were talking business, even when they were here, supposedly having fun.

Whatever. I wanted partner, and eventually, I wanted to be in their shoes. But one thing was for certain. I would never be dull and bland like them. I would be managing partner one day and still live my life the way I wanted.

This was a new era. Love and romance and family and kids...that just wasn't for me.

Celine, my younger sister, could carry forth our legacy if she really wanted.

Even though I knew this shit was passed on from father to son.

But hey, I was breaking the mold, right? Someone had to be a trailblazer.

Give me a glass of whiskey, and I would do that any day.

3

Ava

Belinda Byers personally received me when I arrived at the tall, shiny building where Solomon, Forger, and Riggs were situated.

"You have no idea how glad we are you could start this quick," she said after she shook my hand, and we walked toward the elevators in the lobby together. "We're in desperate need of extra help, and if your resume is anything to go by, you're going to help us out of hot water."

"Are they planning something big?" I asked.

"You didn't hear it from me. I'm sure Mr. Solomon will fill you in once it's underway, but they're taking on a class action. So it's all hands on deck."

"Oh, that's serious," I said.

Belinda nodded. "About as serious as they get. But nothing they do here is half-assed. The managing partners are all sharks. They get what they want, and they have enough money to make sure the resources are in place. It's a pleasure to work with companies this well-funded. It means we can win no matter what."

I nodded. I knew all about poorly funded law firms. I'd worked for a law firm where the resources had been limited because of their funding. It meant they couldn't afford specialist witnesses, research only went so far, and when the opposing council had more resources, it wasn't a matter of right or wrong, it was a matter of who'd been able to prepare the best.

We climbed into an elevator and rode to the forty-seventh floor. When we walked through the tall glass doors, Solomon, Forger, and Riggs had been mounted against a wooden paneled wall in large silver letters. Everything in the office was shiny and polished, with glass walls showing off every office, plush carpets all the way through, and wooden desks polished to perfection.

"This is your office," Belinda said.

My name had already been sandblasted on the glass door.

Ava Brooks, Paralegal.

It looked so professional. A large desk dominated the middle of the office, with large windows overlooking downtown Seattle.

"You'll spend most of your life in here," Belinda said with a smile. "I'm not kidding, either. You're going to have to work yourself to death to prove yourself."

"I'm ready for duty," I said.

"Good," Belinda said. "Follow me."

I walked with her to a full kitchen, complete with five microwaves, a full-sized stove, sub-zero fridge, and an array of coffee machines lined up along one wall.

"You're welcome to leave food in the fridge as long as you label it. But we also have a cafeteria downstairs with a great build-your-own sandwich bar. All the coffee you can drink whenever you need, but don't spend too much time here. If you can work and eat simultaneously, then do that."

I nodded. It sounded like it would be a tough pace to keep up with, but I was determined. Especially if they were planning a class action suit—I wanted to be a part of that.

Two people walked into the kitchen, dressed in suits.

They stopped talking when they saw me and looked me up and down. I was self-conscious, but I'd dressed the part, and I knew I looked like I fit in as long as I acted like it.

"This is Wyatt and Neil, two of our junior associates," Belinda said, introducing me. "This is our new Paralegal." We all shook hands. "Wyatt works with Noah Forger."

"Oh," I said. "That must be interesting." I wasn't sure what to say. The man had a reputation for being a ladies' man, and I knew he was a good lawyer, but I didn't know so much about him.

"I guess that's one way to put it," Wyatt said with a smirk.

I wasn't sure what that meant.

"I have a meeting in five," Neil said, glancing at his watch. "See you around, Ava."

He left, and Wyatt made himself a cup of coffee. We left the kitchen, and Belinda walked me back to my office.

"If you need anything, you can find me down the hall and to the right. But anyone around here will help, just ask. You'll find we're a tight-knit little family—don't let all the fancy finishes and big money fool you. If you do your job well, and you make sure you know where to be and when, you're going to be just fine."

"Thank you."

"I put a file on your desk for you to go through, and then you can jump in. Good luck!"

She left my office, and I was alone. A few employees walked past the glass walls of my office. It was going to take some time getting used to working out in the open like this, with only the two walls on the side closed, and the front of my office all glass. It made me think of a fishbowl, but I could get used to it.

I could get used to anything if it meant there was light at the end of the tunnel.

I sat down at my desk and opened the file to dive into what I needed to do as quickly as I could.

After a couple of hours of undisturbed work, someone walked through my office door. I glanced up from the work I'd been taking care of. I froze when I saw him.

His dark blond hair was stylishly messy, and his baby blue eyes rested on my face. He had a charming grin on his face, and his cologne wafted into my office, bringing back memories of a night between the sheets, his hands on my hips, his tongue in my mouth, and a call that never came.

"What are you doing here?" I asked.

He grinned. "I work here."

"You're Noah *Forger*?" I asked, putting two and two together.

"Finally figured out who I am, huh?"

I blushed violently, and I was immediately furious.

"You didn't call me."

"Sorry. Something came up."

I gasped. "Yeah? Did you forget how to be a decent human being?"

He frowned. "Come on, it's not like we had something special. It was one alcohol-fueled night."

"That's not the point," I said. "You broke your word."

"Ah. That's a thing with you, huh? Okay, mental note made." He grinned at me.

It only pissed me off more.

"Don't mock me," I snapped. "I can't believe this! You're...everything they say you are."

"Handsome, rich, well-endowed—"

"An ass."

He laughed. He thought this was funny. I felt like I could die of mortification, but to him, this was a damn joke.

"Can I help you?" I asked tightly, standing up from my desk.

"I just wanted to welcome you to the firm," he said.

"Thanks."

"If you need anything...I'm sure there are people around here who will help you."

"Kind of you to offer," I said.

"And if *I* need anything, I'll know exactly who to come to."

"And I'll be sure to add you to the long list of things I have to do."

When I said that, his eyes twinkled. "I'm on your *to-do* list, huh?"

I rolled my eyes. "You're a pig."

"Hey, I'm not the one who said she wants to do me." He grinned.

I was furious immediately. It was true what they said about him—every single word. He was a pompous ass who thought he could get away with murder because women would fall down at his feet in worship. And I was willing to bet they did just that.

I'd done it, too. But that had been in a different life, when everything I'd known had fallen apart. I wasn't the same woman anymore.

And I sure as shit wasn't going to accept the same from him.

"Thank you for your warm welcome. I have work to get to, so if you don't mind..."

Noah didn't budge. He folded his arms and leaned against the glass.

"I'm sure you can afford to take a break. Have some coffee with me. Has someone shown you the kitchen?"

"Belinda already showed me," I said. "I'm going to take a rain check on that coffee."

"Come now. You know how this is supposed to work. You're supposed to get on my good side." He waggled his eyebrows at me.

"I would..." I tilted my head sweetly. "I'm just not sure you have one."

The laughter in his eyes faded, and he pursed his lips together.

"I have to go," he said.

I nodded. He paused as he waited for me to try to stop him. But I needed him to walk away from me so I could take a breath and process how the hell the man I was working for was the same man I'd slept with one drunken night a year ago.

Noah clenched his jaw, and damned if that didn't only make him that much hotter. He looked like he wanted to say something, but he caught himself. His lips were parted, and *holy shit*—his lips were full and kissable and perfect. I would know. I couldn't help but stare at them.

Focus, Ava.

When I forced my eyes back to his, his pupils had dilated. The anger was gone, replaced by something a lot more dangerous. Something carnal. So, he was thinking about that night, too.

The air shifted between us, growing thick. What would it be like if he kissed me again right now? Would his arrogance and charm taste as good as it had that night?

His eyes slid to my mouth for just a second, making me wonder whether he was thinking about kissing me again, too.

I cleared my throat and sat back in my chair, breaking the spell. The last thing I needed right now was to get caught up in this crazy déjà vu on my first day at the office. I couldn't afford one misstep. I needed this job more than I needed attention, more than I needed sex.

Even if it came in a package as delicious as Noah Forger.

The fact that he had me thinking about sex at all pissed me off even more. But with a body as great as his and a track record in bed I could attest to, how could I not think about it? I'd thought about it for a long time after he'd left my house, a long time after I'd realized he was never going to call.

"You're sure about forfeiting that coffee?" Noah asked in a husky voice that made me melt.

I swallowed hard, forced myself to keep my composure, and nodded.

He nodded curtly. "Fine. See how well it bodes for you to look for shit with *me*." It might have been worrying if those words didn't come with such a sexy smirk.

He spun around and left my office. The moment he was gone, I sagged against my chair. My heart fluttered in my throat.

"Ava, if you have a chance—" Belinda cut herself short as she walked into my office a moment later. "Are you okay?"

"I'm pretty sure Noah Forger is going to fire me," I said.

"For what?"

"For basically telling him he was an ass." It sounded petty saying it out loud because there was more to the story than she could ever know.

"Someone should put him in his place. I'm glad you did it—he can't stand being treated like anything other than a god."

Now that Noah was gone, and I was left in the wake of his destruction—because with a face that hot, and cologne that intoxicating, what he left behind could *only* be defined as destruction—I wished I'd handled the situation differently.

I always thought of better ways to handle a situation after the fact. In the middle of it, I acted on impulse, and that got me in trouble.

Add regret and a healthy dose of overthinking, and I could work myself up into a panic with ease.

"Will it get me in trouble?"

"Don't stress about it. His dad is the Forger with leverage right now, not him. And Archie was the one who okayed hiring you. Noah can't do anything to you. He just has to nurse his bruised ego. He'll bounce back by tomorrow. Or later today if a short enough skirt walks past."

"You're sure?" I asked. The idea of him looking at other women made me feel sick. I pushed the thought away. I had no right to think about anything. It was my mistake that I'd thought he was genuine. A man that looked like him never was. Stereotyping? You bet. But I had experience.

Belinda nodded and giggled. "I wish I could have seen you take him on. It must have been a sight for sore eyes."

I didn't know how to answer. I was still trying to regain composure.

"What did you want me to look at?" I asked meekly.

"Oh, yeah, here." She offered me another file—like I wasn't drowning in paperwork already. "Just see if you can get this back to me soon."

I nodded. "I'm on it."

"Great. Is someone waiting for you at home?"

"My mom," I said.

"No kids, no husband?" She glanced at my hand, looking for a ring. I shook my head.

"Good, for the next couple of months, you'll be married to your job. You'll eat, sleep, and breathe law. It's good you have the time to dedicate. It's a grueling schedule around here, but the upside is the overtime's good."

She grinned at me and left my office so I could get back to work. I sat down behind my desk again and tried to focus on the work in front of me.

I couldn't stop thinking about Noah. Where did he get off being so demanding? He had no right to be—he didn't own me. But he had no right to be so damn *attractive,* either.

I squashed the little voice that suggested I *wanted* him to be that demanding. If the tension between us was anything to go by, getting back into the bedroom and horizontal beneath him would be something of a fantasy—

Stop it.

I forced myself to focus on the work in front of me. I had to get as much done as I could. Even if it meant sleeping in my office.

Because Belinda had said the overtime was good.

And I needed that now, more than ever.

When I finally got home, it was almost midnight.

"You're still up," I said when I found my mom at the kitchen table, drinking a cup of warm milk.

"I couldn't sleep," she said. "I think it's because I sleep so much during the day."

"As long as you get some sleep," I said and walked to the kitchen table to hug her before I sat down, too.

"How was your first day, honey?" Mom asked.

"It was good. Stressful, but it always is."

"Are your coworkers nice?" she asked.

I nodded. "Very." Noah flashed before me, and my stomach tightened. Thinking about him offered a wave of need, followed by a wave of frustration. But he was every bit as gorgeous as I remembered.

Not that it allowed him to be an ass, which he clearly was.

I shook off the thought of him and told my mom how things had gone, leaving out the part where Noah Forger had cornered me in my office and gotten me all worked up for no reason.

When mom finished her milk, she put her cup in the sink.

"I'm going to try this again," she said with a smile. "You should get some sleep, too. You're going to struggle if you start off the week getting so little sleep."

I nodded. She was right.

We walked to our rooms, bade each other good night, and I got undressed and climbed between the sheets.

I closed my eyes, and let out a slow breath, trying to calm down. But despite being dead on my feet and being so tired, I couldn't fall asleep. My mind kept running over everything I'd done today, and everything I would have to work on tomorrow. I couldn't switch off.

Slowly, my mind moved from work, and I started to think about the people I'd met.

Noah Forger, in particular.

I hadn't wanted him to come any closer. I hadn't wanted to be nice to him, because I liked him. And there had been no alcohol involved this time.

A lot more than I wanted to admit. Something about him was magnetic. It had drawn me in, and despite my frustration with his attitude, I'd wanted to give in to the primal need that had grown at my core.

Just thinking about him now brought that same need back. It unfurled inside of me, making me hot and bothered. Heat warmed me from within, washed over my body, and pooled between my legs.

I closed my eyes and ran my hands over my body. I thought about Noah when I did it. I remembered the feel of his large hands on my back, on my hips, on my breasts... I cupped my breasts and squeezed my nipples through the thin tank top I wore to bed. I arched my back, turning myself on more and more as I thought about Noah's lips on mine, his hands on my body—how he ground his cock against me. I wanted him to hold me close and nibble my neck, lick a line along my collarbone, and kiss his way onto my chest. I gasped softly, picturing how he'd push my tank top up, cup my breast, and suck my nipple into his mouth. I vividly remembered the feel of his hot mouth on my skin, branding me.

I squeezed my nipples, and shivers ran down my spine.

In my mind, Noah was here with me on my bed again, pressing the length of his body against mine. His cock was hard, pressing up against my stomach, and he bucked them, rubbing himself against me as his hands, and his mouth worked magic on my breasts.

Slowly, he made his way down my body, planting kisses down my ribs, my stomach, and down between my hips until he closed his mouth over my pussy.

I pushed my hand into my pajama shorts, and my fingers found my clit. Slowly, I rubbed myself in small circles. I envisioned Noah between my legs, those piercing blue eyes glancing up at me while he licked and sucked on my clit. I imagined him pushing his fingers into me.

I turned my head into my pillow to muffle the sound and moaned softly.

My thoughts shifted to having Noah on top of me, naked. His body was chiseled and sculpted, and the feel of his hard muscles—my bare breast against his chest and his cock buried inside me—sent electric shocks through me. I rubbed my clit faster and faster, as in my mind's eye, Noah drove his cock into me harder and harder. He fucked me so fast that my breasts jiggled and heat spread over my body. My skin flushed as pleasure erupted at my core.

I orgasmed against my fingers, tilting my hips upward, rubbing myself hard and fast as I rode out the pleasure.

The orgasm hit me hard and fast, and it subsided just as quickly.

Because it wasn't really Noah. And it could never be Noah.

I couldn't allow myself to go anywhere near him, in reality. Not again—that would be looking for trouble.

But in a fantasy world, where nothing was real anyway...I could dream about him a little longer.

I turned on my side and closed my eyes. The release had finally switched my mind off, and I was calm now. It didn't take long before I sank into a deep sleep.

But Noah's face was still there at the edge of my consciousness.

I couldn't go near him, I reminded myself.

Even if I really wanted to.

4

Noah

"Are you fucking kidding me?" I stood in my dad's office for two weeks, staring at him. Who the hell did he think he was?

"Don't take that tone with me," Dad said. "I'm sick and tired of your antics. You didn't do what I asked you to do, so now I'm laying down the law."

"I didn't do anything!"

"It's all over the news, Noah," Dad said.

He was right. It *was* all over the news. I'd had too much to drink, and I'd been pulled over. It wasn't such a big deal, though. I'd been two blocks away from home, and everyone at the station were my friends. But some journalist had followed me around and caught a photo of me talking to the cops, and that had made the news.

"No one knows that I was drinking," I said. "And there wasn't a woman in my car. I was alone. Isn't that what you wanted?"

"That doesn't matter. The fact is that enough is enough. Your name is directly associated with our firm. It doesn't take a rocket scientist to figure out how this works. So, you settle down and get a wife, and *then* we'll discuss making partner."

I shook my head, still reeling after he'd dropped the bomb on me that I didn't just have to sober up. I had to *get hitched*. "You can't make me marry someone."

"No, you're right. But I can stop you from moving up in your career until you decide to settle down and get serious about life. Those are my terms—if you don't get yourself a wife, and settle down into family life, you're not going any further than being a senior associate. You're lucky I'm not firing you from the firm."

"That would have been easier," I grumbled.

"The door is open, Noah," Dad said, pointing toward his office door. "You're more than welcome to leave if that's what you want."

I shook my head. I didn't want to leave. Damn it, this firm was my legacy. I was born into a bloodline of lawyers. Walking away from it now would be throwing everything away. Sure, there was no doubt someone else would take me—a lot of law firms would jump at the chance to have me on board. But that wasn't the point.

"What if I don't want to get married?" I asked, sinking into the chair that was facing my dad, seated behind his desk. "It's not in the cards for me."

"I know Adele did a number on you," Dad said, his face softening. I hated hearing her name. I hated anyone talking to me about her. "But you can't hold on to that forever. Shit happens, but you made it out in one piece."

"Yeah, and I learned from my mistakes," I said. "Which means I'm not walking that road again. You and Mom have been together too long for you to know what's out there anymore. The women don't want me, they just want my name, my money."

Dad shook his head. "Not everyone is like that. I found love, so did a lot of other Cavaliers."

I snorted. How many of the men in our club had marriages that were just about arranged by their parents?

"I'm not walking that road," I said firmly. "I'm not going to find someone."

"There's someone out there for everyone," Dad said, shutting me down. He'd been gentle a moment ago, but his business face was in place, and he was going to damn well get what he wanted. "You just need to get your priorities straight."

I shook my head. I didn't care what Dad said about love and family and tradition and all that shit. I couldn't do it.

What about me? What about what I wanted?

Once upon a time, I'd wanted all of that. When I'd met Adele and fallen for her as hard as I had, I'd been ready to lay it all down, get married, have a bunch of kids. I'd been willing to follow in my dad's footsteps in every way possible. But that was before I'd realized women only wanted the money, and they didn't give a shit about me. Adele had gotten money and the future name from me, but she'd found everything else she wanted with another man.

And that hurt like a bitch.

I'd gotten out with my heart in shreds, but I'd managed to patch it back together, and there was no way I would risk doing that again—no matter how much Dad told me there was someone for everyone. I was glad he had a good relationship with my mom, but it wasn't in the cards for the rest of us.

Especially not for someone like me.

"My career is everything," I said. "You can't take it away from me so you can force me to do what you need me to do."

"It's my call, son," Dad said.

"It's not only your call, you have partners," I pointed out.

But I knew it wasn't like that. The three partners stuck together like glue. They were all Cavaliers too, and if my dad said I wouldn't get a promotion, they would support him no matter what.

"Is that all?" I asked when Dad didn't answer me and stood. "Can I get back to work now?"

"Sure," Dad said.

I walked to the door and pulled it open. Before I stepped out, Dad called me back.

"Don't try to look for loopholes, Noah. There aren't any."

I grinned at him. "There are loopholes everywhere. Why do you think I'm so good at my job?"

"Not in this case," Dad said.

I laughed and shut the door behind me, walking away from my dad's office.

The smile on my face slipped away quickly. Because he was right—there were no loopholes when it came to my dad expecting me to change my tune and get *married*.

What the hell was he thinking? He was screwing with my legacy. I was supposed to be in charge of this company one day. But if I didn't get married, I would be a senior associate for the rest of my life.

Nothing about that screamed Forger.

Fuck, fuck, fuck.

I barged into the kitchen and yanked open the fridge, looking for something—anything. But the answer to my dilemma wasn't going to be in the fridge, so I slammed the door shut again. Anger burned beneath my skin, ringing in my ears. My whole world came crashing down on me. Adele wasn't even in my life anymore, but the hell she'd created for me just came back to bite me in the ass again and again.

It was long enough ago that my anger should have disappeared. How long did it take to get over something like that? It had to be simple.

But this was the rest of my life. She'd screwed someone else, and in the process, she'd screwed me *over*. And it just kept rolling, over and over again.

In a way, I thanked her for opening my eyes before I did something stupid and got married. If I had, though, I would be in a different position now...

When I spun around, I nearly ran into someone.

"Hey, watch it!" Ava cried out, bouncing back from the cup of coffee that splashed over her hand. "Damn it!" she grabbed the cup with the other hand and shook off the scalding coffee from her skin. "What the hell is wrong with you?"

I hadn't realized someone was in the kitchen—not that I'd bothered looking before I'd stormed in here.

Coffee had splashed onto her white blouse, making it see-through, and I could trace the lace bra she was wearing through the wet material. I stared. I couldn't help myself—she was hot, with perfect breasts, and a body that screamed to be touched and tasted.

I flashed back to the night we'd shared so long ago, the feel of her body under mine, writhing with pleasure. My cock twitched in my suit pants at the thought of her gasps and moans.

And my anger had gotten the better of me. When I felt like I lost control like this, spinning out with no way to reel it back in, I wanted sex.

Yeah, it was a fucked up vice. But no one in this world was perfect, and I was about as worldly as they got.

"Excuse me," she said tightly, and I glanced up at her. She had a stern look on her face. She'd seen me staring at her chest.

"Do you have any manners at all?" she demanded.

"Well, yeah," I said. "Sorry." I grinned at her. Okay, so I grinned in bad situations, too. It only made things worse, but damned if I could help myself. I *never* played poker, for the record. That was one brand of gambling that just didn't work for me. But with Ava...I was more than willing to take my chances.

"That might have been nice if you meant it," she snapped.

"Come on, I'm sorry. I didn't mean to make you spill your coffee, and I didn't mean any disrespect." I offered her my most charming smile.

"Yeah, you did," she replied and walked to the sink. She washed the coffee off her hands. "You're nothing but disrespectful to the women around you. You forget that I know you."

I bristled, my latent anger still threatening to break free. But it wasn't aimed at her, and she didn't deserve it. "You don't know shit about me..."

"Okay, tell me you're not an egotistical asshole who gets whatever he wants, sleeps with women to get off, and never calls back after sex." She pinned me with a hard glare.

I opened my mouth to argue, but she was right.

"I thought so," she said when I shut my mouth again.

"There's more to me than that, you know," I said softly.

I walked to her and picked up a washcloth. I gently pressed it against her neck and chest.

She rolled her dark eyes up at me. God, what I would give to see those dark eyes rolled up at me like that with her lips around my cock. I had her on her knees in front of me, once. I wanted it again.

Something about her was magnetic, and I wanted all of her. I couldn't describe what it was—I'd wanted women before, but not like this. I never did a repeat. I slept with them once, and that was it. Otherwise, they got the wrong idea.

But I wanted Ava. Again and again and again.

What the hell am I thinking?

Her breath caught in her throat. Her lips were parted, and her eyes locked on mine. She was fractions away. I could lower my head and kiss her right now. I could drive her back, lift her up onto that counter behind her, so that she could wrap her legs around my waist.

My cock stirred in my pants just thinking about her. Her hot breath in my ear, her back arched...

Stop it.

"Is there?" she asked. Her voice was breathy, and she sounded a lot less collected and upset than a moment ago. She swallowed hard and took a step back, breaking the spell. "I've heard the stories around here, you know. They say you think you're everything. And maybe you are, since you're a Forger. But your name doesn't mean you get a hall pass to being a dick to everyone around you, and they'll just let you off the hook."

As she spoke, her voice steadied again. She was angry. Her eyes spewed fire. I was aware of how her chest heaved, her breath coming faster. And it made her so damn hot. I wanted to grab her and kiss her. But she would probably slap me for it.

Feisty as fuck.

I loved it. And she didn't want anything to do with me. She was immune to my charm. Which just made me want to win her over that much more. I'd managed once, hadn't I? I'd never been around a woman who wasn't interested in hooking up—everyone wanted a piece of this so they could either get the bragging rights or hope for a longer term situation where they could cash in.

I'd also never been with a woman I couldn't get out of my head like Ava. The combination was a bad one.

"You're right," I said.

She blinked at me. I'd caught her off guard. Good.

"I was a dick, and I'm sorry." She wasn't going to get any kind of confession out of me. I just wanted her to give me another chance. God knows why, but there it was. I was Noah Forger. I acted on impulse.

"So, let me try again. Go out on a date with me."

"You're still telling me what to do."

Damn it, couldn't she just give in, already? I groaned. "Will you go on a date with me?" There, was that better?

She tilted her head to the side, thinking about it. And if that wasn't the damn cutest thing I'd seen in a while, I didn't know what was.

She shook her head.

"I don't date people in the office."

"That's not an office policy," I said. Or was it? I wasn't even sure. But if it was, it shouldn't be.

"It's *my* rule," she said.

"Maybe I should just have you fired. Then there will be no strings attached, and you can go out with me without worrying about your rules." I cocked a grin at her.

She pursed her lips together, and a smirk crossed her features. It was the closest I'd gotten to a smile from her.

"You see, I would have trembled at that idea, but word around here has it that you're not the Forger with clout. The one who hires and fires is your father. So, you can't do anything to me."

I stared at her. The mention of my father, his position, and my *lack* of it, brought the anger right back. I wasn't even good enough around here to hire and fire. I was nothing but a lackey, hiding behind a good name and an expectation I could never fulfill.

Damn it!

"If you'll excuse me, I have to change my shirt," she said and turned around, leaving me reeling alone in the kitchen. She had no idea how her words had just gutted me, reminding me that I was nothing, and never would be anything, unless I gave up...everything. Who I was, what I wanted. What I needed.

A part of me wished I'd handled her differently from the start so that I could get through to her. The more she pushed me away, the more I wanted her. But another part of me didn't want to give in. I was Noah Forger, and I got what I wanted.

Always.

Except Ava, apparently.

But I'd had her once before. I could do it again. I just needed a bit more time.

5

Ava

I found a dry shirt in one of my cabinets—since I'd started working overtime, I kept fresh clothes in my office. I'd worked through the night on a project more than once.

With my clean shirt in hand, I walked to the ladies' room. As soon as I was inside, I leaned against the door and let out a breath I didn't realize I'd been holding.

It had been almost impossible to turn Noah down. Those eyes of his were mesmerizing—I could fall into those eyes forever if I wasn't careful. And despite being set on hating him, I was so damn attracted to him I couldn't think straight. It was easier being angry at him, so that I had a reason to push him away. Otherwise, who knew what I would allow?

Especially when he was trying to be nice, and didn't just believe his charm was enough to do the trick.

I shook my head and walked to the sink. I took off my shirt and splashed cold water on my chest and face. It helped to cool me down after Noah had me all hot and bothered. The way he looked at me made me think of all kinds of things I shouldn't have been thinking.

Like what it would be like to kiss him again. Like what it would have been like for him to touch, kiss, and lick me.

What it would be like if I let him fuck me again?

I just had to remember who he was. It infuriated me that he thought he was the be-all and end-all of the universe. Kyle hadn't thought he was the center of the universe, but he'd thought he was the center of *my* world, and that had been bad enough. I was so sick of men acting like they were better, expecting me to fall at their feet in worship. It irritated me and made it hard to see redeeming qualities.

And I'd taught myself to stop searching for them so desperately, and see the red flags for what they were.

As long as I reminded myself that he believed he could have whatever he wanted just because he was a Forger, then I could keep him at arm's length.

That was all I had to focus on.

He hadn't called me back the last time we'd played this game, after all. The only reason he was in hot pursuit now was because I wasn't interested. The moment I gave in, he would forget about me again.

I couldn't deal with it a second time. The first time had been embarrassing. Now, it would be downright pathetic.

After changing into a clean blouse and checking my hair and makeup in the mirror, I composed myself. I took a deep breath and left the ladies' room to go back to my office. To my relief, Noah wasn't there, waiting for me. If he pushed me now, if he did anything that remotely turned me on, I would let him kiss me.

And then I would be in trouble. I couldn't afford for him to do even that.

I sat down behind my desk and focused on my work. I still had so much to do today, I would have to work overtime yet again.

But overtime meant more money in the bank by the time my first paycheck from Solomon, Forger, and Riggs came in, and maybe it would be enough to buy us another month in our home.

When the phone rang, I jumped.

"Ava Brooks," I answered.

"Miss Brooks," a male voice said on the other end of the line. "This is Steven Heath speaking."

My stomach dropped. "Mr. Heath, how are you?"

"I'm doing you a favor by calling to find out where you stand with your finances."

"I don't have it yet," I said. "I just started a new job, but I won't get a paycheck until the end of the month. If you can just give me a chance—"

"I'm sorry, Miss Brooks," he said, interrupting me. "I can't give you another chance. I've given you multiple extensions all year. It's out of my hands at this point."

I shook my head and dropped my head into my hand.

"You do realize that this debt isn't our fault, right?" I asked. "We didn't get ourselves into this position. It was—"

"I'm well aware of the situation, Miss Brooks," Mr. Heath interrupted me. "But the law is the law. You understand how it works, don't you?"

I sighed. If anyone understood the law, it was me.

"You have a week to vacate the property. If you don't, the bank will arrange for it to be done for you, and we can't guarantee where your possessions might end up."

A lump rose in my throat. My skin burned, and my blood rushed to my ears. How was I supposed to tell my mom that I'd failed? That she was going to lose the home she'd lived in all her adult life?

The line went dead. Mr. Heath had ended the call, not even bothering to say goodbye. He didn't care about what would become of us. He only cared about getting back what my dad should never have given in the first place.

I put the phone back in its cradle and took a deep breath, trying to compose myself. But tears stung my eyes, and sobs racked my chest no matter how hard I tried to suck them back in.

I had to do something—was there nothing at all I could do?

My mind spun. Would it be possible to ask them to give me an advance on my paycheck? God, it was the most unprofessional thing in the world to ask for. And after only working here for two weeks...

I grabbed a pen and started scribbling on a piece of paper.

Dear Mr. Solomon, would it be possible to give me an advance—

I crossed it out, scribbling angry lines through it, before I tried again.

Mr. Solomon, I know I haven't worked here for very long but—

There was no way I could do this. Who would listen to me? Who would grant me an advance?

I sighed and scribbled again.

I'm losing the house. I couldn't make all the money I should have. I failed.

"I hope you're looking down from wherever you are and realizing what shit you dropped us in," I said softly. Not that my dad would be able to hear us now.

"Ava, do you have a minute?" Neil asked, popping his head through my door. "I need your help with a case."

I nodded and stood. I took a deep breath and put on a brilliant smile, surprising even myself at how well I could slip my mask into place. I would need it next week, when I had to come into the office from God knows where—possibly after sleeping in my car.

Paige had asked me what I would do when it came to this, and I'd told her I would deal with it when the time came. I'd known I might not be able to make it happen. I'd known we could get to this point. All I had to do was take the next step. As soon as I had a chance, I would look around for an apartment. Even though I didn't have a security deposit or money to rent a moving van, or anything else.

I pushed the thoughts away. I wouldn't think about that now.

One step at a time.

When I walked into the conference room where a bunch of junior associates scratched their heads about a legal question they had, I was ready to tell them how to make it work. Because no matter what, I still had this job, and that counted for something.

6

Noah

When I walked into the office on Monday after a weekend of drinking, my head ached, and I wasn't in the mood for this shit. But I had cases to win and a father to prove wrong, and damned if I was going to go down without a fight.

He didn't think I was worthy of making partner because of my lifestyle choices. But I won every case I worked on for the firm. I brought in a lot of clients—not promoting me would only be bad for the company.

I was going to tell him that, too.

On my way to his office, I heard a cheer from the boardroom.

I frowned and stopped. All my colleagues were there, lifting champagne glasses into the air. When I stepped into the boardroom, Nick Mueller came to me. He pushed a glass of champagne into my hand.

"I'm glad you made it! I thought you might be even later than usual, so we started without you."

"What are you talking about?" I asked. "What are we celebrating?"

"I just made partner," Nick beamed. "Looks like the old men upstairs finally cracked and gave me what I've been working for all these years!"

He lifted his glass in the air, and behind him, the other guys cheered again.

Richard Stephenson came up behind him, throwing his arm around Nick's shoulders.

I'd started as an intern with both of these guys. Nick and Dick. It had been a running joke until he'd punched someone for it. I'd been promoted faster than them twice. And now...Nick had just left me in the dust.

"Can you believe it?" he asked me. "None of us believed we would make partner before you do. Looks like they're not as fucked up as we thought, huh?" he burst out laughing, clapping Nick on the back. "And here we all thought the old men were playing favorites since you're a Forger."

Nick and Richard laughed loudly.

I bristled. Nick was partner!?

I forced a smile and sipped the champagne. It was bitter in my mouth, and didn't taste like victory at all.

In fact, it tasted like a giant loss. What the fuck was going on here? Nick wasn't partner material. No way they wanted him at the round table, one of the *knights* that represented this firm as a partner. This was a shot aimed at me.

Directly.

My dad had probably roped Zeke and Maurice in to promote Nick so that it would rub salt on my already smarting wound.

And it was working, too. I was pissed off as hell.

"Come on, don't be such a sour puss," Richard said, noticing when my smile slipped again. "We're all in this together, eh? We all work as hard as you do, if not harder."

"I'm not a sour puss," I said through gritted teeth. "I'm happy for you. Really." So happy, I could punch him in the face. But it wasn't Nick who was trying to make my life hell. He was just a pawn in my dad's games—proof that my dad was still in charge, ruling my life even though I was thirty-one and more than capable of making my own decisions.

God, sometimes I hated this life. I loved being a lawyer. I loved the cash that came along with it, but I hated how my dad still had the final say in who I was and what I wanted to do with my life.

From the outside, being a Cavalier was coveted—everyone wanted a piece of what we had. They saw money; they saw fame; they saw people who had everything they could possibly want in the world.

But from the inside, this system was rotten to the core. All I could do was what my dad wanted. We were all stuck in the same game, just at different levels. Being a Forger meant I was just as tied up as the rest of the guys. My name was one of the biggest names in the club, in the firm...in the country. And there was no freedom in that.

All the money in the world couldn't make up for the fact that I would forever be defined by what my father wanted for me.

I drained my champagne glass.

"Well done, Nick," I said. The words were hard to say. I wasn't happy for him. I didn't think he deserved it. "You're going to be great." More lies, but I couldn't be a sore loser, could I?

I turned around and left the boardroom.

"Where are you going?" Nick and Richard both called after me.

"I have a case to take care of. Sorry boys, duty calls."

It wasn't a lie. I had a ton of work to get through before the end of the day. My mind spun, my ego was severely bruised, and anger prickled my skin. The only way I could make this happen was if I kept working as hard as I did, giving my dad no way to keep holding me back. He couldn't cut me down if I worked as hard as I did, right?

Wrong.

He would do what he wanted, when he wanted, no matter what. But what else was I supposed to do?

It wasn't like I could buy myself a wife—money went far in this world, but there were limits. Even for a man like me.

I needed to get the hell out of here before I did or said something stupid that would let them know exactly how fucked up things were. The last thing I needed was for word to spread around the office that my dad had me under his thumb, and there was nothing I could do about it. That would just make me look about as pathetic as I felt right now.

Ava wasn't in her office when I stormed in. Her door was open, her laptop on, but she was probably somewhere helping the junior associates get their shit together for their seniors. I hoped she was helping Wyatt—he wasn't the best junior associate I'd ever had. I could do without him, with the workload I had to take over, anyway. He could use all the help he could get.

I stared at her desk. I'd dropped a file off in her office last week that I needed her help with—I was looking for a legal loophole to get my newest client out of hot water for something that was very much his fault. I'd noticed over the past three weeks of Ava working here that despite being as cold as she was toward me, she had a hell of a mind on her. She was damn good at her job. As if she wasn't already attractive enough. As beautiful and sexy as she was—she was smart, too.

Something about her made me want her in every way possible. She was the whole package.

And she wanted nothing to do with me.

I tried not to think about that. My ego was already dented enough after my dad's little stunt. I didn't need to be reminded that Ava was the one woman in the world I wanted who didn't want me back. Which only made me want her that much more and made me sulk like a child that I couldn't have her.

I rifled through the files on her desk, flipping them open, going through stacks of papers. I needed that damn file. I doubted it hadn't been done yet. Ava knew what she was doing, and if I knew anything about her work ethic by now, she'd had it done almost before I'd delivered it to her.

A piece of paper fluttered to the floor. I bent down and snatched it up, turning it over to read what it said. It was written in her handwriting, with various sentences scratched out. But I could still read them.

Dear Mr. Solomon, would it be possible to give me an advance

Mr. Solomon, I haven't worked here for very long, but

I'm losing the house. I couldn't make the money I should have. I failed.

"What are you doing here?" Ava asked from the door.

I jerked and turned to face her. Her eyes slid to the note in my hands.

"What's that?" As she realized what I was reading, her face paled, her eyes widening. "What the hell are you doing in my stuff?" She'd meant for it to come across as irate, but her voice was breathy. She took a few steps toward me and snatched the note from my hand, crumpling it up into a ball as if that would negate that I'd seen it at all.

"So, losing the house, huh?" I asked.

She bristled. "That's none of your business. You can't snoop around my office like this. I should turn you in to HR—"

"I can help you with the money."

"What?" she asked.

A plan formed in my mind. I wasn't this good at my job for nothing—thinking on my feet was the name of the game. She needed something, I needed something. Turned out money *could* fix everything. If she agreed.

"Marry me."

She gasped. "What!?"

"I need a wife. My dad is a pain in the ass and won't promote me unless I'm married. And you need cash. So, I'll pay you. Be my wife. I'll squash whatever financial issues you have."

"And you don't think your dad is going to wonder how the hell you're suddenly married?" she cried out.

I shrugged. The more I thought about it, the more perfect the plan seemed. I couldn't believe I hadn't thought about it before. Man, I was good at thinking on my feet.

"He never told me *how* I should get a wife. Just that I need to get married if I want that promotion. It looks to me like it will be a win-win."

She narrowed her eyes at me, her face twisting in a mask of rage. God, she was so fucking hot when she was angry. I could just imagine what angry sex would be like with her.

Ava glanced over her shoulder toward the office floor, to see if anyone had heard what I'd just said.

"I'm not marrying you for money," she said, lowering her voice.

I shrugged again. "The offer stands, but not for long. Think about it. I'll give you two days."

"There's no need to give me a deadline. The answer is no," she said firmly.

I grinned and glanced at the crumpled piece of paper in her hand.

"Like I said, think about it."

I left her standing in her office, looking like she'd just been railroaded.

I hoped to God she would take the offer. If she needed the money as badly as it seemed, then this would work out perfectly for the both of us. And I could just imagine the look on my dad's face when he learned that I'd gotten married just to make him give me what I wanted.

But it wasn't just about that. If she was married to me, it would give me a chance to get closer to her, to figure out what was behind that icy wall she had up all around her. I wanted to get to know her. Fuck if I knew why, but I wanted what I wanted.

If I was lucky, I would learn she was just like everyone else, and the strange hold she had on me would finally break. I could stop thinking about her, stop wanting her.

And we would still both have what we wanted. My dad had told me there were no loopholes, but he had no idea exactly how good I was at my job.

I was the king of loopholes. It was how I won every case.

And my dad was about to taste my wrath. I just needed her to play along.

And something told me that she would.

7

Ava

"I can't believe this place is so full for a Monday," Paige said when we walked into our regular bar.

"Maybe they all have sorrows to drink away," I said dully.

Paige shook her head. "It's not that bad, Ava. Really."

"Yeah?" I asked. "I'm losing the house in a week."

Paige nodded. She couldn't say anything to that.

"Unless I do something crazy."

"Like what?" Paige asked with a frown. "You're not going to do something stupid, are you?"

I burst out laughing and swirled my Apple Martini in the glass.

"I think losing the house because I didn't do absolutely everything I could, might be the stupid thing."

"What are you talking about?" Paige asked. She sounded concerned. "What's going on?"

I glanced at her. "Noah Forger wants me to marry him."

"What!?"

Her response was exactly what I'd expected it would be.

"For money," I added. "He found out about me losing the house, and he needs to prove something to his dad, so he asked me to marry him. He'll take care of all my finances if I do."

Paige looked horrified. "And then?"

"And then..." I shrugged. "I don't know. I guess we'll be married. But my mom will still have the house, and she'll be taken care of. And that's all I want. She doesn't deserve what my dad did to her."

"Neither do you," Paige pointed out. "But you can't sell your soul like that."

"What choice do I have?" I asked. "I don't have anywhere else to turn. I've worked my ass off since the day my dad passed away, and we learned about this debt, but it wasn't enough."

"Then lose the house," Paige said simply. "I get that it sucks, and it's stability that's being taken away from you, and your mom is in a bad place because of all this...but you can't tie yourself to someone like him for the rest of your life. People who don't marry for love...it never ends well."

I giggled. The alcohol was already going to my head. The whole thing sounded so stupid, so crazy, so *ridiculous*. It was funny.

"It's not funny," Paige said, as if she could read my mind. "It's serious."

"I know," I said, my smile fading. "And I'm serious, too. My mom can't afford to lose the house. She's not mentally stable. I can't let her spiral into depression even more. You've seen what she looks like these days. Sometimes, I can't even get her out of bed. If she gets worse than she is now, I worry about what will become of her. And it's not like this is a permanent thing."

Paige stared at me.

"Marriage *is* a permanent thing, Ava."

I shook my head. "It doesn't have to be. Everyone gets divorced these days, right? It will just be one of those. Everyone will think 'oh, it didn't work out' and then I can move on with my life. I just...I need a clean slate, P. You have no idea how hard this is. I'm so damn tired of worrying, of not being able to sleep, of working so hard and never getting out on the other end of all this."

Paige wanted to argue with me, but there was nothing she could say. She didn't have loads of debt. She didn't have a mother to take care of. I worried day and night that my mom would one day decide to check out of the hellish life my dad left behind for her. And I couldn't afford to lose her on top of everything else.

Losing the house would make her spiral to a new level, and that scared the living shit out of me.

So, what if I had to pretend to be someone's wife for a while?

"You can't do this," Paige said again. "I know it's tough, but this is your life, Ava. You can't throw it all away for the sake of money."

I groaned and finished my drink. It was easy for her to say because she had enough money to get by, and she knew what was coming for her. She didn't have to do any kind of damage control, she didn't have to clean up someone else's mess.

Maybe she was right. I couldn't afford to sign my life away for the sake of money. But now, being up to my eyeballs in debt, it was hard to look at everything objectively.

"Another?" Paige asked, raising her glass.

I nodded. "I shouldn't, but yeah, another. I should be at the office, working. But since I'm not doing that, might as well hit me with a good dose of alcohol so that I can stop thinking altogether."

Paige grinned. "You work way too hard, Ava. It's good to let your hair down once in a while."

She ordered her first, and yet another martini for me.

"In other news," I said. "I got a text from Kyle again."

"Are you serious?" Paige asked. "What did he say?"

"He just said he wanted to meet for coffee. As friends. I didn't even reply. I don't have time for that on top of everything else. And there's no way he just wants to be friends."

"Men never want to be friends after dating."

"They barely want to be friends *before* dating," I pointed out.

Paige laughed. "Good for you. He's full of shit, anyway."

"Men generally are," I said and lifted my glass. Paige lifted hers, too, and we clinked the rims together before the topic changed to other things. Paige told me about a guy she liked in her office, about how they flirted with each other, but if he didn't make a move sometime soon, she was going to stop waiting for him to do something.

I liked listening to her babble on. It took my mind off my own troubles for a while. It wouldn't last long, though. The moment we left the bar, my troubles would come rushing back at me to hit me in the face over and over again.

But whatever. I would escape for as long as I could.

By midnight, I was sufficiently drunk, and Paige called it quits.

"I have to be in the office at six tomorrow to organize Dan's flight," she said.

"Dan is your boss, right?" I asked.

My words slurred a little.

Paige giggled. "How drunk are you? I've only worked for Dan for about five years, and talked about him just as much."

I shrugged. "Sorry. Alcohol makes me fuzzy."

Paige nodded, and we paid our bill before she stood to leave.

"You should go home and get some sleep," she said gently. "You have a long week ahead of you."

She was right. I had to pack up my house, prepare my mom for the fact that the rug would be ripped out from underneath our feet, and try to do it all in between the hectic work schedule I had at Solomon, Forger, and Riggs.

Paige hugged me. "It's going to be okay. You know that, right?"

I nodded and hugged my best friend back. But I didn't believe that it would be okay. It didn't feel like it.

"Are you coming?" Paige asked.

"I'm just going to have a glass of water or something, before I leave, too," I said. "If I don't try to sober up before I get in bed, I won't make it through the week."

Paige nodded. "Okay, get home safe. Let me know when you do, so I know I don't have to come here and scrape you off the sidewalk or something."

"Elegant visual," I said and flashed a grin.

Paige giggled, blew air kisses at me, and left the bar.

I sighed and sat back in my booth, watching the patrons coming and going. I tried to imagine who they were and what they did. What were their lives like? No doubt, it was easier than mine. I imagined they didn't have so much debt; they weren't losing their homes; they were here a lot more carefree than I was.

Someone appeared in front of me. I stared up at him. It took me a moment to realize it was Noah. He looked different without his suit—he wore jeans and a collared shirt, with loafers and an expensive watch on his wrist.

He looked delicious.

"What are you doing here?" I asked.

"I came out for a drink," Noah said. "I was working until now. Can I join you?"

His arrogant façade was missing. He was just a normal guy.

Or maybe I was way too drunk and missed out on the red flags waving in my face.

I nodded, even though I wanted to tell him to go away. He was half the reason my life was a mess right now—how could he tempt me with money by offering me something as obscene as getting married for it?

He sat down. "What are you drinking?"

"Water, I'm too drunk for more alcohol," I said.

Noah shook his head. "Have one drink with me."

"I'm not drinking with you. The last time I did that, I ended up...it will be a mistake. You have no idea what's real..."

Noah laughed. "Yeah? How's that?"

"Do you know how serious marriage is? Do you know what it's like to be in love and to want to spend the rest of your life with someone because you can't imagine being without them?"

He gave me a leveled look.

"I know what it's like to want something desperately enough to put it all on the line."

His eyes were deep and his face serious—he really meant what he was saying.

Noah lifted his hand and brushed a strand of hair from my face. His fingers grazed my cheek and sent sparks of electricity through my body.

"Why are you doing this to me?" I whispered.

"I'm not doing anything *to* you. I'm doing something *for* you."

He was wrong. He wasn't doing this for me. But if I did this, it wouldn't be for him, either.

His eyes slid from my eyes to my lips, and he inched closer and closer. I should have pushed him back—he was everything I wasn't interested in. Pompous, arrogant, infuriating. But he was so damn hot, too. And the way he looked at me set me on fire. He wanted me. And the truth was I wanted him, too.

The tension between us grew thick and I couldn't help but stare at his mouth.

When he leaned in and kissed me, I kissed him back. A little voice at the back of my head screamed at me that this was a bad idea. I was going to get left behind again. This was Noah Forger—we were co-workers. He was my boss's son. We'd walked this road before, and it had hurt more than it should have. I had every reason in the world not to allow this to happen.

But the small voice drowned in alcohol and carnal need, and when he slid his tongue along my bottom lip, without a question, I opened my mouth and let him in.

He pulled me tightly against him, and devoured me. His lips pressed against mine, and heat washed over me. My core tightened, and the need to have him inside of me was suddenly overwhelming.

When he broke the kiss, I gasped.

"Let's get out of here," he said.

I nodded.

He threw a wad of money onto the bar and stood, taking my hand. I let him lead me out of the bar, and to a cab waiting on the curb as if the driver knew we'd be coming out at that exact moment. I vaguely wondered what had happened to the car he'd called the last time we did this.

Noah opened the door for me, and I climbed in. He followed and gave the driver his address.

His, not mine.

Noah put his hand on my thigh, and his hand branded my skin. He slid it higher and higher up until his fingers brushed against my crotch.

It was familiar. His touch was déjà vu. Being with him was a memory.

It was like coming home.

My breath caught in my throat.

When we stopped in front of a fancy high-rise, Noah paid the driver with another stack of cash, and he helped me out. I leaned on him. The alcohol made it hard to balance on my heels.

He led me into the building, past the doorman at the reception desk, and into the elevator.

The doors slid shut, and Noah turned to me. He pushed me against the elevator doors, his head on my neck. I gasped and moaned when he nibbled the delicate skin on my neck, grinding his erection against me.

He was as horny for me as I was for him.

"We shouldn't do this," I murmured.

"But we're doing it anyway," he mumbled in response, planting kisses down my neck and on my chest.

The doors slid open again, and Noah led me to his front door. He pushed it open, looking around.

"What are you looking for?" I asked.

"I'm just making sure we're alone."

"What?" I asked. "Why wouldn't we be alone? You're not in a relationship, are you?"

Noah rolled his eyes. "God, no. Not unless you want to be." He waggled his eyebrows at me. My stomach twisted, but I squashed the feeling. Right now, I didn't want to think. I just wanted to feel.

Noah kissed me again. Now that we were alone in his apartment, his fingers found the hem of my shirt, and he pulled it up. I helped him, lifting my arms. He dropped the shirt on the floor and cupped my breasts. I moaned when he squeezed and massaged my breasts. He peeled the lace cup down and tweaked one nipple between thumb and forefinger.

Noah ground his cock against me, driving me backward until the dining room table was behind me. He moved onto my chest, kissing a line of fire down my neck. With expert hands, he unclasped my bra. When he pulled it away, he sucked a nipple into his mouth. I gasped and pushed my fingers into his hair, curling them into fists. He groaned when I tugged at his hair as he worshipped my breasts. I melted into my panties as he kissed and sucked, closing my eyes to the pleasure.

He worked his way down my body, planting kisses over my ribs and stomach. His fingers found the buttons on my pants, and he undid them before slowly peeling them down my legs. He took my panties with them, and in no time, I was naked on his dining room table.

It was sinful, and such a turn-on.

My thighs fell open for him, and Noah wrapped his arms around my legs. I laid back on the cold, lacquered wood and closed my eyes. The world felt like it was tilting on its axis with the alcohol in my system. I wrapped my fingers around the edge of the table and held on.

When Noah closed his mouth over my pussy, I gasped. He parted me gently with his tongue, licking slowly at first up and down my slit. He flicked his tongue faster over my clit. I shivered and moaned, arching my back, writhing on the table as he pushed me closer and closer to the edge.

Pleasure rippled through my body, and my skin felt like it was on fire. The closer I got to an orgasm, the louder I moaned. Noah was very in tune with what I was feeling. He pushed me closer, and listened to my breathing, backing off when I got too close so that he left me teetering on the edge.

I moaned in protest. I ached for the release.

Noah plunged two fingers into me, and I cried out when he sucked and licked my clit while finger fucking me. I gasped and moaned, and a moment later, the orgasm rocked through my body. I closed my legs around Noah's head, breathing shakily as I rode out the orgasm that started at my core and washed out to my extremities.

When it was over, I gasped at the table.

Noah chuckled, looking at me with glistening lips.

"You're still dressed," I gasped.

"We can't have that," he said and grabbed his shirt behind his neck. He pulled it over his head in one swift movement.

I stared at him. He looked even better than I remembered. He was built like a god, with muscles rippling under his skin, every inch of him perfect, as if he'd been carved by angels.

I pushed myself upright and fiddled with his jeans, undoing them. I reached into his pants and set his cock free. He was thick and long in my hand. When I pumped my hand up and down, Noah groaned and sucked his breath through his teeth before he grabbed me and kissed me again.

I wanted him inside of me. I wanted him to take me to his bed, get on top of me, and pin me down again and again as he fucked me.

As if he knew what I was thinking, Noah picked me up. I wrapped my legs around his waist, and he carried me through the apartment, kissing me as we walked to the main bedroom.

He dropped me on the mattress of a large, king-sized bed, and kicked off his jeans. He paused only for a second to roll a condom onto his cock before he climbed onto the mattress with me.

He kissed me again, and I wrapped my legs around his waist. He pressed the tip of his cock against my entrance, and I held my breath in anticipation. When he slid into me, I moaned against his lips as he speared me. My body stretched to accommodate him. He braced himself with his arms on either side of my head and started pounding into me. I gasped and moaned and cried out, my breasts jiggling as he fucked me harder and harder.

Another orgasm racked my body, and I shivered and trembled around him. My pussy clamped down on his cock, and Noah groaned through gritted teeth. I gripped his shoulders, my nails digging into his skin, holding on as if I would float away if he didn't anchor me.

When I came down from my second orgasm, Noah wrapped his arm around my body, pulling me tightly against him. He rolled over, and I yelped when he pulled me onto him.

I straddled his hips, and gasped at his size—a new challenge at this angle.

I braced my hands on his chest and started bucking my hips, riding him. Noah's eyes were locked on mine, his brows knitting together. He clenched his jaw, and as I rode him, he grunted and moaned in rhythm with my fucking.

He gripped my hips, helping me ride him faster and faster, pushing deeper into me, and pulling back further.

My clit rubbed against his pubic bone as we fucked, and yet another orgasm grew at my core.

It didn't take long before I toppled over the edge again, and when I orgasmed, I cried out and collapsed on his chest. Noah still had my hips in a vice grip, and he fucked me from beneath, hard and fast and with urgent strokes.

He shoved himself into me as far as he could, and his cock jerked and twitched as Noah groaned and bit out cries of ecstasy.

We cried out in unison, riding out our orgasm together.

Finally, when it subsided, I lay on his chest for a while longer, listening to his heart hammering against my cheek.

I slid off him, his cock slipping out of me. Noah sat up and got rid of the condom before he laid back down again.

"You're fucking incredible," he gasped.

I blushed, smiling at him. It had been *amazing* sleeping with him, doing all of this again when I'd told myself I wouldn't go there with him, again. It had been better than I'd thought it would be—better than I'd allowed myself to dream it would be.

And I'd thought about it a couple of times over the last few weeks.

He turned to me, and I rolled onto my side to face him. I stared at his face, tracing the lines of his straight nose, his thick eyebrows, and his high cheekbones with my eyes. His eyes were blue like the sea and I sighed as he ran a thumb gently along my cheek. The man lying in front of me wasn't the same man I saw in the office all the time. He seemed like a robot in the office. Now, he was just human.

"Okay," I said.

"What?" he asked.

"I'll do it. I'll marry you."

Noah's face went from a surprised frown to a happy grin. "Yeah?"

"Yeah. I need the money, and you need the job. It's like you said—win-win. But there are rules."

"What rules?" he asked.

I steeled myself. The rules were there to protect me, because Noah was everything a girl could want, and I could get hurt if I didn't do this right. Getting hurt wasn't a part of my agenda. I couldn't deal with another heartbreak. Not now, when my delicate house of cards already threatened to fall.

"It's only going to be a year. We're not doing this long-term. You have a life I'm sure you want to get back to, and I'm not going to stay in a relationship without love."

Noah thought about it a second before he nodded. "That sounds fair."

"I also need you to help me with my mortgage. Like, right away. We're going to lose the house at the end of this week if we don't figure it out soon."

Noah nodded. "I've got you. We'll take care of it."

"And then I have a ton of debt my dad left behind that I—"

"I've got that, too."

I hated sounding like I was after the money, but that was exactly what this was.

"And we can't do this again," I said.

"What?" Noah asked.

"Sex."

He frowned. "What?"

"You heard me. I'm not here to be a toy. This is a business arrangement, and fucking around like this is not professional."

Noah chuckled. "Nothing about this is professional."

I pinned him with a hard glare. I needed him to understand how serious I was about this. The truth was I *did* want to sleep with him again. But I knew who Noah was—I knew what he usually does. He was Seattle's biggest playboy, and there was no way in hell I was going to fall for this man when he was just getting off with another woman before he moved on to the rest of his life. Because I could easily fall for this man. Everything about him was intoxicating.

"Fine," he finally said. "No sex, all your debts are covered, and a year. Anything else?"

I nodded. "I don't want the whole world to know about this. Not unless it's necessary. The last thing I want is to be a public spectacle."

Noah nodded again. "Fine by me. Makes it harder to get some ass when people think I'm actually married."

I narrowed my eyes at him, and he burst out laughing.

"I'm kidding. But it's fine, we won't tell everyone. Anything else?"

I nodded again. "No big white wedding. I want that for when it's the real deal."

Noah nodded solemnly. "A court wedding it is. I love a woman who gets down to business."

"What about you?" I asked.

"What about me?"

"Don't you have conditions?"

He shook his head. "I'm already getting what I want out of this. We don't need more rules."

"Okay," I said.

"Okay," Noah answered. "And now...we should get some sleep."

I nodded. He was right. We had to get some sleep. Tomorrow was going to be tough at work. And soon, we would get married. I needed all the rest I could get to deal with this.

When I closed my eyes, Noah wrapped his arm around my shoulder and pulled me closer.

"What?" he asked when I glanced up at him. "We're not married yet, so your rules don't apply. And I don't know about you, but I'm a cuddler after sex."

I let him pull me closer. The last time we'd done this, I'd freaked out and sent him away. Now, freaking out wouldn't help. I would be stuck with this man for the next year. And honestly, there were worse things.

It was nice to be this close to him, and I drank in his warmth. I was still a little drunk, and the room felt fuzzy around me.

Right now, I was content to stay lost in the moment.

Tomorrow, I would face my reality.

I'd just agreed to marry Noah Forger.

8

Noah

Aaron and I sat in the car at the airfield, waiting for the girls to arrive. The rain had turned Seattle into a gray canvas. It wasn't a downpour that drenched you in seconds. It was a relentless drizzle that threatened to last four days and seeped into every corner until it felt like the world was drowning.

"Isn't it bad luck to have rain on your wedding day?" Aaron asked.

"I don't think this counts," I said.

"Where are they?" Aaron asked. "They're late."

"I think that's normal. But it's fine, we'll wait."

"We were supposed to leave an hour ago."

I rolled my eyes. "The point of having a private jet is so that it doesn't leave until we're on it."

Aaron nodded and sank further into the leather seat, looking out at the dreary landscape.

"I think you're making a mistake," he said.

I shrugged. No one would understand what I was doing. Aaron had been gracious enough to keep his mouth shut about it. I needed a witness. And between him and Gunner, he'd been free.

"I'm doing what I need to do," I said.

"Yeah, you explained that to me. But you know your dad is going to lose his shit about this, anyway. It's not going to work."

"We'll see," I said and grinned at the thought of my dad finding out what I was doing. My dad was black or white on matters, with no gray areas. He stuck to the rules, he played the game the way it was meant to be played, and he couldn't accept anything that wasn't followed to the letter.

In this case, that letter would be his ultimatum, and the letter of the law. He told me to get married. He didn't specify how. I was just doing what he asked.

"Did you get everything taken care of?" Aaron asked.

I nodded. "I flew out yesterday to make sure the license is done, and the paperwork is ready."

"Not taking any chances, huh?"

I shook my head. "No way. Not with this."

Aaron shook his head, too. He wanted to say a lot, but he didn't. Good. His life wasn't cut-and-paste either. He'd had a bad run-in with a woman a long time ago, and as a single father, the man had just as much baggage as the rest of us. We judged in private, we made jokes when it was okay to do it, and the rest of the time, we didn't say shit when it wasn't our place.

At least, we did it that way most of the time.

"Here they are," I said when a cab pulled up. I climbed out of the car and held an umbrella over the passenger door when Ava climbed out. Her friend followed suit, and Aaron was right behind me.

Ava looked incredible. She wore a plain white dress with a low neckline, and it flared a little around her hips. She wore white ballerina flats with it, and she'd pinned her hair back. Her makeup was classy, too. She might have asked for something simple—she wanted to save a white wedding for when it was real—but she looked breathtaking nevertheless.

Her friend wore a peach dress in much the same style, but the blonde didn't look fit to be at a wedding party. She wore a scowl and sized me up the moment her eyes fell on me.

"This is Paige," Ava said, introducing her friend. Paige gave me the evil eye—I was willing to bet she was against this whole thing, too.

"Aaron," my friend said, holding out his hand to the two women.

"The plane's ready," I said after I paid for the cab, and it drove off. I nodded toward my private jet. "Are you ready to go?"

"Where are we going?"

"I registered us in Vegas," I said. It was the easiest, quickest way to get a marriage license. The only downside was that we had to get married in the county we registered in. But with a private plane, that wasn't a downside at all.

Ava glanced at Paige, who raised her eyebrows.

"Let's do this," Ava said and pursed her lips. She looked determined.

And nervous.

When we were on the plane, the girls sat on one side, and Aaron and I, on the other. Ava looked distracted. She glanced around the plane, and I tried to see it through her eyes. Everything was white leather, with polished chrome accents and lacquered oak finishes. Hopefully, she would see what this meant—I had more than enough money to make sure she was taken care of. We had a deal, after all. The flight attendants offered everyone champagne. Ava took a glass and downed it in one gulp before she took another. This time, she sipped it more slowly.

The plane took off smoothly, and we flew out of Seattle. The rain stopped a moment later, and then the sun broke through the clouds. I caught Ava's eye and smiled at her. She returned it nervously. Her friend kept glaring at me, as if I was forcing Ava into something she hadn't agreed to do. But Ava had agreed to this herself. She'd made the rules.

We were doing this.

We landed in Vegas and got into the black limo that waited for us. I wanted to wow them. I wanted to make a big fuss, make it extravagant. But Ava didn't seem wowed. She just looked nervous as she played with the hemline of her dress.

When we arrived at the courthouse, I took her hand and pulled her aside.

"Do you still want to do this?" I asked.

She nodded. "We have a deal." Her voice was thin.

"I know, but it's not too late to back out."

She hesitated for a second, but then she nodded. "We have a deal." This time, her voice was more determined.

When we turned, Paige stood in front of me.

"Head in," she said to Ava. "I'll be there in a sec."

Ava nodded and took a step away. Paige turned to me, her features stern.

"Look, I know you two have a deal, and Ava is her own person, so I'm going to stand by her whatever she decides to do. But she's been through hell and back more times than I can count these past two years, and she doesn't need you to add to that, okay? Look after her. I mean it."

I nodded. "I'm not going to let her get hurt."

Paige narrowed her green eyes at me.

"I'm serious."

Finally, she nodded and turned away, joining Ava inside the doors to the courtroom. My stomach twisted into a knot of nerves. I was serious when I said I didn't want Ava to get hurt. I would do my part, I would do what I'd promised to do. I hadn't told Ava yet, but I'd already sent the money for her mortgage payment. Even if she had rejected me, I would have had that covered for her—she worked hard, had integrity, and didn't deserve to be thrown out on the street.

No matter which way this deal went.

I would tell her that later, though. I didn't want her to feel forced into this. I *needed* a wife to get what I wanted. But I still wanted to treat Ava right. In the past three weeks I'd seen her in the office, I'd seen a woman who deserved more than what she was going through.

At least, this way, I could give her something. Even if it was small.

But getting married to her...that was the part I was nervous about. Because she was great in every way. She was the kind of woman I could fall for. What if I fell for her, and then she walked away after all this ended?

"Are you ready?" Aaron asked, coming to me.

I exhaled a deep breath and pushed my emotions away. I wouldn't fall for her. I barely knew her. She was just a means to an end.

"Ready," I said.

Aaron nodded, and we walked into the courtroom to get the show on the road.

This was for the greater good. This was so that my dad could eat his words.

If he wanted to make his silly rules, I could play his silly game.

My stomach clenched again, but I shoved the nerves away and steeled myself.

This would work. It *had* to.

ele

When my plane touched back down on the runway in Seattle, I spotted my dad's silver Bentley out in the rain.

"Well, fuck," I said.

"What?" Aaron asked, craning his neck to see what I was seeing.

"Did you tell him?"

"Tell who?" I asked.

I bristled.

"What's wrong?" Ava asked.

I shook my head. "Don't worry about it. It's just my dad."

Ava gasped. "Your dad's *here*!?"

I nodded. My stomach did a loop. I knew this was the only reason he would be here right now, coming to meet us the moment we touched down.

"I thought you said we were going to break it to him this weekend," Ava said hotly.

"Yeah, well, turns out word travels fast."

I glanced at Aaron, who held his hands up in defense. "Don't look at me. I was with you guys the whole time."

"Did you post anything about this?"

"No, I just sent the photo to the group." We'd taken a photo at the chapel of the four of us, and I'd taken a photo with Ava after that. Just the two of us—our wedding photo. I would have wanted to make more of an effort, but she didn't want me to do anything special. Not unless it was the real deal.

And that was fair, actually. Since this wasn't a real marriage, it wasn't right to celebrate it as one.

I narrowed my eyes at Aaron. "You sent it to the group?"

"Yeah, you know, so the guys can see what's going on. We're all rooting for you, man."

"You know Charlie is in that group, right?"

"Yeah?"

"And Charlie is dating my sister."

Aaron's face fell. "Shit, man. I'm sorry. I didn't think—"

"You never fucking think," I snapped. "I thought you, of all people, would have learned your lesson after Samantha."

Aaron clenched his jaw. "Way to bring that up now, asshole."

"You don't get to be pissed at me," I sneered. "*I* get to be pissed at *you*." I jabbed a finger against his chest.

"Everyone, just calm down," Ava said. "Archibald was bound to find out at one point or another, right? I mean, that's why we did this in the first place—so he would know."

I nodded. "I just wanted to break it to him on my terms."

"Well, we can't all get what we want, can we?" Paige said tightly.

I glared at her, and she glared right back at me.

"Let's get this over with," I muttered. "Are you ready?"

"No," Ava said. "But we'd better get it over with."

I nodded as the flight attendant opened the door when the plane came to a full stop. I didn't let Ava walk out of the plane first, which might have been the gentlemanly thing to do. Instead, I stepped out first, letting her follow me. It would have been rude of me to send her into the lion's den first.

Dad's jaw was clenched when I stepped down the few steps, and his eyes were murderous.

I flashed him my award-winning grin. "Hey, Dad."

"Don't you dare take that tone with me? What the fuck do you think you're doing?" He bristled, his anger so incredible I expected steam to rise from his skin in the drizzle. My hair had already started to cling to my face.

"You're always crashing my parties," I said.

My dad didn't think it was funny. He glared at Ava, who stepped down behind me.

"Miss Brooks," he said tightly. "Do you want to explain to me what's going on here?"

Ava opened her mouth to speak, but I interrupted my dad.

"That's Mrs. Forger, Dad," I said.

Dad looked like he was going to explode. "What did you do!?" he cried out. "Do you have any idea what this will look like when the news gets out? And you..." he spun around to face Ava again. He struggled to find the words, his anger getting the better of him. "Of all the insolent, pain in the ass, good-for-nothing women Noah has run around with, I didn't expect you to be one of them."

"Sir, I—"

"Don't even think about trying to defend him," Dad said.

"Dad—"

"And you have no right to speak, either!" Dad cried out, cutting me off, too. He looked at Ava again. "You're fired."

She gasped, paling.

"No," I said firmly.

"What?" Dad asked, frowning. My reaction took him aback.

"What?" Aaron echoed. He and Paige had followed us out of the plane, and they'd watched silently as my dad had lost his shit on us.

"You're not going to fire her. And you're not going to fire me, either. This is what you wanted."

"What?" Dad asked, more confused than angry now.

"You wanted me to get married. So, there. I'm married. This is all on you—you pushed for this, and I gave it to you."

Dad stared at me for a moment.

"This isn't what I meant," he finally said.

"You didn't specify." I grinned at him. "Loopholes, Dad. You can't tell me I'm not fucking good at what I do."

"What do you do?" Dad asked coldly. "Because all I keep seeing you do, is fucking up." He glared at Ava. "This isn't over. But I'm not going to stand in the rain and be made a fool of. We'll have a conversation about this later." He turned on his heel and stormed off back to his car.

Aaron whistled through his teeth. "That was intense."

I nodded and turned to Ava.

"I didn't think he was going to take it out on me," she said softly. "I can't afford to lose my job. I can't—"

"Hey," I said, sliding my hand down her arm and taking her hand. "You *can* afford it, because I've got you covered. That's part of our deal. But I'm not going to let him fire you. He's pissed at me, not you."

"Are you sure?" she asked.

I nodded. "Yeah. I'm sure. I'm not going to let him do anything to you."

She nodded, her lips pursed.

"Let's get out of the rain," I said.

We turned to the sleek black car that arrived on the tarmac to take us home.

"Wow," Aaron said when he walked next to me, the girls falling back to discuss what had happened.

"What?" I asked.

"You won't let him fire her?"

"She's not the problem here. This is between me and my dad."

"Yeah, sure," Aaron said, nodding slowly. "But for a moment there, you sounded like you really cared."

I rolled my eyes. "Stop being a dick. This is your fault, you know."

Aaron sighed. "Yeah, I know. But do me a favor, okay?"

"What?"

"Stop bringing up Samantha. I'm so fucking over having to bite my tongue about Adele, but you can mention my ex any day you want?"

I nodded. "That's fair."

"You have way too much shit on your plate to cause even more trouble," Aaron pointed out. "You need all the help you can get in your corner right now."

I chuckled. "You think it's that bad?"

"Bro...I think it's worse."

9

Ava

What did I think was going to change after I married Noah Forger? I had no idea.

But whatever it was I'd expected, going back to life as usual hadn't been it.

I blinked my eyes open. The light that fell into the enormous guest bedroom that had become my bedroom in the penthouse suite was still a light gray, proof that the night had only recently faded away.

It was still early.

I sat up and rubbed my eyes.

This room was fit for a queen. All the rooms in Noah's penthouse were large enough that one would fit our living room, dining room, and kitchen at home, and they were decorated as if we lived in a lavish resort. Noah hadn't really thought to give the guest room a personal touch, but it was luxurious all the same.

And judging by the way he was never home, he didn't have to. This was just a place to rest his head and nothing else.

I stretched under the silk sheets and sat up, rubbing my eyes. I strained my ears, listening for movement in the apartment. Noah's soft snoring came from the room next to mine. He was still asleep.

I climbed out of bed and walked to my bathroom. It was just as grand as everything else in the house—a jet bath dominated one corner, and a waterfall shower took up the far wall. His & Hers basins with a large backlit mirror showed every freckle on my nose, and the floors and towel racks heated during the winter.

Everything about this place was magical.

I turned on the hot water and stepped into the spray, letting the hot water run through my hair.

I'd been living here for about a month now. The weekend after Noah and I had gotten married—I was still getting used to saying that—I'd moved in here. Noah had insisted that I stay here if we were going to convince his dad that we were doing this for real.

Not that I thought Archibald was fooled for one second. The old man knew exactly what was going on, what Noah was capable of, and he was still furious with his son. And with me.

At least, he hadn't fired me. I still worked at the firm, and even though Archibald Forger refused to speak to me unless he was forced to, my work there carried on as if not much had happened.

Noah hadn't been promoted, though. He was pissed about that. But what did he think his dad was going to do, roll over and show his belly?

As different as the two Forger men were from each other—Archibald the old school, and Noah the new school—they still had a lot in common. One of the most obvious things was their stubbornness.

My mom didn't know I was living with Noah. She didn't know I was married. I'd told her I was moving in with Paige so that I could be closer to the office with my long hours. I visited her twice a week, and once over weekends, and I sent her money whenever I could.

When I'd told her we weren't losing the house, she'd started coming out of her depression.

Now, when I saw her, she smiled more. She didn't sleep all day away, and she got out of the house to go for walks sometimes. We still had a long road to walk—she wouldn't get better overnight. My dad was still gone, and he'd left us with a legacy of lies and deceit that we still had to work through on top of mourning his loss. But one step at a time would do the trick.

And before we know it, the year here with Noah would be up, and I would be back home with my mom, too.

Or maybe, since we would be in a much better space financially, I could get an apartment of my own.

I would decide closer to the time.

After I showered, I dressed in a black knee-length pencil skirt, a button up white top, and I pinned my dark hair back and out of my face. I put on leopard-print kitten heels to complete my business casual look and tiptoed out of the bedroom.

Noah's door was ajar, and I snuck a glance in.

He was laying spread-eagled on the bed, one arm hanging off the mattress. His light hair was disheveled, his bronze skin unblemished except for a small arrow tattooed on his left tricep.

And he looked edible.

God, sometimes I wished I hadn't made the rule that we couldn't sleep together. Sometimes, I just wanted to go to bed with him, and wake up next to him. Some nights, when he was in the kitchen putting a meal together, or at the bar mixing drinks, a part of Noah that he didn't show the rest of the world shined through. His arrogant mask slipped, and I saw a pensive, serious man underneath.

He always pulled that mask into place so quickly again when he realized I was looking. But I wanted to get to know that side of him.

Not that I had the feeling Noah would ever allow something like that. He seemed hell-bent on keeping everyone at arm's length. Including me.

Especially me.

But it was better that way. Noah was a self-centered jackass, and I couldn't afford to fall for his soft side just because I thought he had the *potential* to be different. I would just get hurt in the process. I didn't know him very well, but what I did know about him was enough to tell me that getting involved with Noah would only get me burned.

I had enough trouble to deal with in my life. I didn't need a broken heart on top of everything else. Not when we both knew this agreement had never been made to last.

While I stared at him, Noah blinked his eyes open. His eyes were a piercing blue, and I jerked back out of sight when I realized he was looking at me. He'd caught me staring.

I backed away from his door, spun on my heel, and quickly walked to the kitchen where I started up the fancy coffee maker.

I tapped my foot to no beat in particular, waiting for the machine to start, before I pushed a mug under the nozzle and programmed it to make me a cappuccino.

Noah walked into the kitchen a moment later, wearing only a pair of boxers. My cheeks warmed, and I forced myself not to stare at him.

"Morning," he said, and I could hear the smug grin in his voice. Damn it, I'd probably stared him awake like some creep.

"Coffee?" I asked.

"Sure," he said.

I nodded, and when the machine finished filling the cup, I handed it to him.

"It's cappuccino," I said.

"Oh." He took it from me. "You like it strong, first thing in the morning, huh?"

I blushed hard. Why the hell was I blushing like this?

"I like to start with a bang."

He laughed out loud at that. I shook my head and forced a smile, although I wished the earth could swallow me up. What the fuck did I just say?

"I have to go," I said. "I need to get to the office."

"Come on, have breakfast with me."

I shook my head. "Some of us have to work for a living. I can't afford to get in as late as you do."

"Sure you can."

"Your dad will fire me."

"We'll just tell him we shared the marital bed." He waggled his eyebrows and grinned. "He can't find fault with that, now that his son is married, and the sex is actually something that comes with the job description."

I bristled. "Except that it's not."

He shrugged. "Yeah, well, he doesn't have to know that. Come on, babe."

I shook my head and walked past him to leave the kitchen. Despite not being showered or dressed, he smelled *good*. How did he do that? I bet the SOB didn't even get morning breath. He was a god among men.

The problem was that he knew it. And his arrogance was a personality flaw.

But he made even *flaws* look good.

I shook off the thought and left the apartment quickly, before he could change my mind. I tried to focus on all the tasks ahead of me while riding down in the elevator to the basement parking. Noah had gotten the management to allocate me a parking spot even though they were full. I got in the car and peeled out of the parking garage, turning toward the office.

The sooner I got to the office and buried myself in work, the sooner I could get Noah out of my mind. I shouldn't have let myself even stare at his almost-naked body to begin with. And the fact that he'd caught me...

Could anything be more mortifying?

It was a good thing my mom didn't know what was really going on. She believed in true love—even after what my dad had done to us—and nothing about Noah could be classified as love. Lust, on the other hand?

Oh, there was plenty of that going around.

10

Noah

The Cavaliers were all at the club, and the mood was just how I liked it. I sat on the leather couch I usually occupied and puffed on a Cuban cigar. Aaron actually drank for a change next to me, and Gunner was on his fourth whiskey.

It was going to be a good night.

"Where's Ben tonight?" I asked Aaron.

"My mom's entertaining him for the weekend."

I nodded but didn't ask anything else. When I had told Aaron to leave my ex out of our conversations, he had asked me to stop bringing Samantha up too. That was only fair, and I didn't want to pry into his personal life too much. Especially if it meant he got out for a change and enjoyed himself.

Behind me, the older men all laughed loudly.

"I'm telling you, the son of a bitch is trying to screw me like he screws the judge!" my dad cried out. By the sound of it, he had more than enough whiskey in his system too. He was laughing and shouting for a change, which meant he was well and truly drunk. Archibald Forger didn't drink very often, but when he did, he gave everyone a run for their money.

"I can't fucking believe it," Landon laughed. "If Brad had to pull half the shit you let Noah get away with—"

"Do you think I'm *letting* him get away with this?" Dad cried out. "Tell me how you would stop Brad from being married if he's already done the deed, tied the knot, the whole parade."

Landon shook his head and laughed.

He was the only one of the older crowd I actually liked hanging out with. He was young at heart. He'd been divorced a long, long time ago, and he'd practically raised most of us Cavaliers, taking us under his wing when the rest of our fathers had been too busy building the legacies we were meant to continue. Not that Landon wasn't one of them—he had the company, he had the money, he had everything that made him fit in.

He was just different.

"I wish I was there, man," Gunner said, tipping his empty glass at me. "Not for the wedding part, but Aaron says your dad was pissed when you got back."

"You have no idea," I said with a chuckle. "But what's he going to do? He can't make me divorce her."

"Has he given you your promotion?" Gunner asked.

I shook my head and sighed. "No, he hasn't."

"Which was the point of this whole exercise," Aaron said. "So, he might not force you to divorce her, but if he still doesn't give you want you want..."

"He has to buckle," I said. "He told me I wouldn't make partner until I'm married, and now I am. Dad can't go back on his word, it's not in him. He's a to-the-letter kind of man. That's what makes him such a good lawyer."

"And you?" Gunner asked. "What makes you a good lawyer?"

"Getting myself out of any situation I get myself into the first place," I said with a grin.

"That sounds more like you *need* a lawyer, not that you're cut out to be one."

"Same thing," I said with a shrug. "You know how it works. We know how to bend the rules because we know the rules."

Gunner burst out laughing and shook his head before he threw back the last of his whiskey.

"Let's get out of here," he said. "Let's hunt some skirts."

Aaron snorted. "You can barely walk straight."

"Don't need to walk straight to fuck straight," Gunner said matter-of-factly. "Are you coming?"

"Sure, I'll come," Aaron said. "I don't get to do this a lot. It could be fun."

"Great," Gunner said with a grin. "What about you, Noah?"

I shook my head. "You guys go ahead. I'm not in the mood."

Aaron and Gunner both froze and stared at me.

"What?"

"You're not in the *mood*?" Gunner asked, narrowing his eyes.

I laughed. "That's not impossible."

"No, but improbable," Aaron pointed out.

"Yeah, well, that was before."

"Before what?" Gunner looked genuinely confused. And I had to admit, it was strange for me to turn down the opportunity to find a woman to warm my bed for the night.

"Before I got married."

Gunner stared at me. Aaron groaned.

"Come on, man. It's not like it's real and you guys are in love or anything. She's just a means to an end." Gunner shook his head.

"Yeah, I know. But it's still not right. What do you think it will look like to the press if it comes out I'm married, but I took another woman home?"

"I thought you kept it quiet for that reason," Aaron said.

I shrugged. "You guys can go ahead. I'll catch up with you next time." I stubbed out my cigar in the ashtray and stood. Gunner and Aaron glanced at each other and shook their heads. They didn't get it, but that was fine. I wasn't going to be the guy who brought home another woman to the apartment while Ava was there. It would make me a total dick. I could be a son of a bitch on some days, but that didn't mean I wanted to fuck with Ava that way.

I didn't give a shit about any of the other women I'd had in my life. Most of them had been nothing more than entertainment for the night, and I couldn't even put names to their faces. Ava was different. But I wasn't about to pull it apart and analyze what I felt for her—that could only lead to trouble.

"I'm out," I said.

"Where are you going?" Dad asked from behind the couches at the bar.

"Home," I said.

"Alone?" Landon asked.

I only shook my head and left.

None of them got it. And sometimes, I didn't get it, either. But whatever. It didn't matter—what they thought didn't matter.

Right now, it wasn't like I was getting what I wanted, no matter what I did. At some point, I had to accept the fact and move on with my life. I just didn't know what the hell else I would do. My life was only about one thing—getting what I wanted. And now that I couldn't...

I got in my car and drove to the apartment building. I rode the elevator up to the penthouse and unlocked the door.

Pop music played from the surround sound speakers inside, and when I walked into the living room, Ava stood barefoot on the rug, a glass of wine in her hand, swaying to the music. Her eyes were glued to the view of the Seattle skyline.

I watched her while she moved, not sensing my presence. She was beautiful. Natural.

She was everything every other woman I'd been with could never be.

When Ava turned and saw me, she froze.

"I didn't realize you would be back so early," she said, and switched off the music.

"Don't stop on my account," I said.

She shook her head. "I should get back to this paper. I can't figure out what to do with it."

"What is it?" I asked.

"It's just a case for Belinda."

"Let me have a look," I said. "Maybe I can help."

She hesitated before she nodded, and we walked to the dining room together, where a bunch of papers was scattered across the tabletop.

"It's a mess," she said.

I picked up the closest piece of paper, and frowned, pulling out a chair. Ava sat down next to me and leaned in. I liked having her this close. I could smell her shampoo and her perfume, subtle after a long day.

"Okay, tell me what you've already got," I said and turned to face her.

Her face was so close to mine, it was almost impossible not to kiss her. But I bit back, because it was her rule.

Fucking rules.

She glanced at me, and for a second, her eyes were filled with want. But she slipped a mask into place and sighed before she started telling me what the case was about.

11

Ava

When Noah stopped trying to put on a face and act like he was the biggest guy in the room, he was a pleasant person to spend time with. *Really* pleasant.

I explained to him what I was stuck with, and he didn't talk down to me or treat me like I didn't know what I was talking about just because I was a paralegal. It was what I'd expected from him.

But lately, he surprised me more often, giving me something different from what I expected of him.

A while ago, he'd told me that I had no idea who he really was. I was starting to believe that that was true on a lot more counts than I realized.

"This stuff is just driving me crazy," I finally said after we'd been working it out for two hours. I scrubbed my hands down my face before pressing one hand to the base of my neck. "I'm just going in circles, now."

"Maybe you should take a step back and forget about it for a while," Noah suggested, putting his hand on my shoulder. "If you stop thinking about it altogether, the answer might come to you."

"Yeah? Is that how you do it?"

He grinned at me. "Why do you think I go out partying and drinking as much as I do? It's all a part of the job."

I laughed. "Only you can make it sound like you're on the clock when you're out there having fun."

Noah's hand was warm on my shoulder, and he massaged me, his strong fingers working at the knots I'd been cultivating night after night bent over court documents.

"You're tense," he said.

"I know." I dropped my head, my hair hanging in front of my face like a curtain. "I have so much going on."

"Turn," Noah ordered, and I shifted in my seat so that I sat sideways on it, my back to him. Noah put his hands on my shoulders, and he dug in deep. I groaned as he massaged out the knots, his hands making magic on my tense shoulders. He shifted closer on his chair, his legs wide around my chair, and gently he nudged me back so that I leaned against him. His chest was solid, and his body warm. I closed my eyes and relished in the feeling of my muscles releasing the tension of the day.

Noah's breath was in my hair as he slowly massaged and rolled his thumbs along my shoulders.

He pressed his lips against my temple. A shiver ran down my spine. We weren't supposed to get this close. I'd laid down rules for a reason. But his closeness was soothing, and his expert hands on my shoulders lulled me into relaxing more than I had in a long time.

I didn't stop him.

"You work too hard," he finally said. "You should take some time off."

"I can't afford to," I said, turning my head toward him.

"Of course, you can," Noah said. "I took care of your bills, and debts, and you're making a ton of extra cash from me, aside from your job. You can absolutely afford to take time off."

He was right. I had a lot of money, now. But I was putting most of it away for when this was all over. The marriage arrangement wouldn't last forever, and when that day came, I wanted to have more than enough money to pull us through if something else went wrong. I wasn't taking chances with finances. I would never allow us to be in a bad situation again.

It was bad enough that my dad—the person who should have taken care of us—had put us in this situation, and he'd lied about who he was and what he was doing. He'd deceived us, betrayed us.

If it wasn't for Noah, I didn't know what I would have done. But he wasn't going to be around to pick up the pieces for me forever.

"It's not that simple," I finally said. I rested my forehead against Noah's cheek, drinking in his closeness. I couldn't explain to him why it wasn't that simple—someone with as much money as he had, with no care in the world, just wouldn't understand.

Noah didn't ask, either.

Instead, he moved his hand from my shoulder to my chin and gently tilted my face up to his.

"I've got you, Ava."

His eyes were steady, intense, and I fell into his gaze. When he lowered his head to kiss me, I didn't fight him. I had every reason not to let him do this. We were married for convenience, not for love. I'd worked it all out in my mind.

I'd just forgotten to account for things like lust, like romance, like being inexplicably drawn to Noah no matter what I did to resist.

I closed my eyes and gave into it. Everything felt right with Noah. Everything worked. It made no sense. He was an ass, and I had to keep him at arm's length. But he was acting like less and less of an ass the more we got to know each other.

Pushing him away right now seemed pointless. Not when he was caring and gentle and sweet. He didn't make me feel like just a conquest or a good time. He made me feel like he respected me as a paralegal who worked with him, and he cared for me as a person.

Noah's hand slid slowly from my shoulder onto my breast. He held me, his hand hot through the t-shirt I was wearing. I sighed into his mouth.

He kissed me, his tongue parting my lips and exploring my mouth, while he squeezed my breast. Heat ignited at my core, and a need for him erupted inside me.

I broke the kiss and sat up.

"We shouldn't do this," I said.

Noah sighed, but he nodded. "Yeah, you're right."

I cleared my throat and stood, stacking the different files and papers together so that I could take them back to the office after the weekend.

Noah hovered close by. I was hyper aware of his presence.

I turned to him after clearing up the table, my work now in a neat stack.

He was close enough for me to reach out and touch him. His eyes filled with longing, and I couldn't read the expression on his face.

"I don't usually do this, you know," he said.

"What?"

"The same person. More than once."

I laughed. "You're painting such a beautiful picture."

He shook his head. "I'm not trying to be rude or whatever. I'm just saying, I don't usually spend time with someone long enough to get to know them. I don't do conversation, I don't do affection, I don't do repeats because that leaves questions I'm not ready to answer."

I nodded, pursing my lips together.

"I understand."

"You don't," he said, shaking his head. "I'm trying to tell you that with you. I *want* to do this. And I don't know why. You scare me, Ava."

I blinked at him. "I don't know what to do with that information."

He shrugged and pushed his hands into his pockets. For a moment, we stared at each other. The ache for him inside me grew stronger, and the need for each other stretched thin between us.

Finally, I gave up trying to fight it. I gave up reciting my rules to myself again and again.

I stepped forward, pushing our bodies against each other, and I pressed my lips against his.

Noah immediately cupped my cheeks and kissed me. Hard. I wrapped my arms around his neck, and he slid a hand down my back, grabbing my hip. He pulled me tightly against him and ground his hips so that I could feel the full length of his erection. He wanted me as badly as I wanted him.

I lifted his shirt and tugged it over his head in one smooth motion. We broke the kiss, and Noah pulled up my shirt, too. Slowly kissing, touching, undressing each other, we made our way to the bedroom. We dropped items of clothing on the floor as we went along, fumbling with buttons and zippers, stumbling over each other.

I ran my hands over Noah's naked torso, scraping my nails down his ribs. He unclasped my bra and cupped my naked breasts, my nipples erect in his palms.

By the time we made it to his bedroom, I was only wearing my panties, and he was naked. His cock stood at attention, thick and commanding.

I pushed him so that he sat back on the mattress, and sank to my knees between his legs. He groaned when I dropped my head into his lap and sucked his cock into my mouth. I bobbed my head up and down, taking him in deeper and deeper. I devoured him, trying to satisfy the carnal hunger that had opened inside of me.

Noah pulled me up after just a few pumps.

"You have no idea how fucking good you are at that," he said in a hoarse voice. "But I want to be inside of you."

He pulled me onto the bed with him and pulled down my panties. His hand found my clit, and he fingered me while I moaned deeply. He rolled onto me, and my thighs opened up for him. He held his cock and ran the head up and down my slit, teasing, before he pushed into me. I gasped when he filled me to the hilt.

He started moving his hips faster and faster, pumping hard and deep. The friction pushed me to the edge of pleasure in no time.

"Wait," I gasped. "You're not wearing a condom."

"Fuck," Noah bit out. "I hate fucking condoms."

"Me, too," I admitted.

He groaned and rested in me for just a moment longer before he pulled out. I pressed my hand to my forehead and closed my eyes while Noah rummaged for a condom in his nightstand drawer.

When he climbed onto the bed again, he was wrapped up. He plunged into me without ceremony, and I cried out as his cock drove into me again. He fucked me harder and harder, bucking his hips, and the sound of our sex filled the room. Moans and gasps punctuated the rhythmic slap of our hips against each other.

I ran my hands over Noah's back and curled my nails into his skin. He clenched his jaw and cursed through gritted teeth.

"You're driving me crazy," he said, and he pounded into me harder.

When the orgasm exploded inside me, I cried out loudly and curled my body around Noah. I rode out the waves of pleasure as he slowly stroked in and out of me.

I collapsed underneath him, gasping.

Noah didn't ask me to change positions, he didn't ask me for anything kinky. He stayed on top of me, his eyes locked on mine. He dropped kisses on my face, and his gaze was filled with affection I was scared to dissect.

When he started moving again, his movements were slow and sensual. If I didn't know any better, I would have thought Noah was getting attached to me, with the way he stared at me.

I ran my hand through his thick, sandy hair. I traced his jaw with my finger. I committed this look on his face to memory. I had a feeling I wouldn't see it soon again. Tonight, we were breaking the rules. We were looking for trouble. *But it could be an isolated incident,* I told myself. It was just sex.

Even if it didn't feel like it.

When Noah picked up the pace, I stopped thinking altogether and gave myself over to the feeling of him inside me, stroking in and out faster and faster. He kicked into a new gear, his strokes shortening. Another orgasm built inside me, but his fucking now was for his own release.

I orgasmed, and a moment later, Noah groaned and dropped his head into my neck. His body trembled on top of me, and his cock spasmed inside of me as he released.

I ran my nails over his back, and he shivered and groaned in my ear.

The pleasure that rocked through us felt like it connected us, pulling us closer together. And for a short moment—so fast that I wasn't sure it was real when it was gone—I felt like we were so close, I didn't know where he ended, and I began.

When we came down from our sexual high, Noah rolled off me. He sat up, and breathed hard. I closed my legs and rolled onto my side.

He planted a quick kiss on my lips before disappearing into his bathroom. When he came back, he was sans condom, and he dropped himself onto the bed.

"Come here," he said, and pulled me closer to him.

I lay on his chest, listening to his heartbeat slowly calm again, until it beat at a normal pace and his breathing had evened out.

"Everyone thinks that sex is all I care about," Noah said into the darkness of the room. "I guess I created that image for myself."

I nodded. I didn't speak, and Noah kept filling the silence.

"Not a lot of people know that I wasn't always this way. I was really serious about someone, once. I was ready to get married, have kids...all of it."

"Really?" I asked, surprised.

"Yeah. Hard to believe, right? But it's true. I was young and stupid back then."

"What happened?" I asked.

"She slept with someone else."

My heart ached for him. That had to be hard—relationships at a young age were already so tough. It was the first of everything, and it meant so much. To then have someone you cared about sleeping with someone else...

"I'm sorry," I said.

Noah nodded, and we lay in silence for a while.

"Why are you telling me this?" I asked.

He turned his head to face me, and I glanced up at his blue eyes, navy like the ocean in the dark of the room.

"I'm not the womanizing asshole everyone thinks I am. I don't care what they all think of me—it's easier when they know what to expect from me. But I just wanted you to know that it's not just about that for me. It's just..." his voice trailed off.

"Safe," I said.

He blinked at me before he dropped a kiss on my head. I settled on his chest again. He didn't have to justify himself to me. It meant a lot that he felt the need to tell me. And it made me see him in a different light.

Why did he want me to see him differently? I tried not to think about it too much.

Finding the answer to that question would complicate everything, and I wasn't sure I was ready for that.

Noah stroked my hair, and my eyes started to droop, exhaustion finally taking over.

"I should probably go to bed," I whispered when Noah's breathing deepened, too.

Noah shook his head. "Stay," he said.

"Are you sure?"

He responded by squeezing my shoulders.

I should have gone to my own bed. I should have followed through on my intentions to keep things simple. But I was warm, and being in Noah's arms was comfortable. I didn't *want* to go back to my own bed.

So, I closed my eyes and took a deep breath, letting it out slowly. I could be tangled up in Noah for a while longer. It wouldn't cause more damage than sleeping together might have done, any more than leaving would fix the fact that I'd broken my rule and slept with him again.

Tomorrow, I will dissect the feelings that rose inside me. Tonight, I just lived in the moment with Noah, and let him hold me.

12

Noah

"It's been way too long since we did this, man," Aaron said.

I nodded. "It feels good to let loose. Split." I glanced at the dealer who split the two nines he'd just dealt me so that I could play them separately.

"Is your dad getting off your case about your drinking and gambling now that you're married?" Gunner asked from my other side.

I snorted. "No. He still sees me as this kid who needs to be guided and schooled, not a grown man. I can do whatever I want with my money, I keep telling him that. But I think deep down, he still sees it as *his* money."

"Well, the money in the trust fund is."

"Sure," I said, watching the cards the dealer laid out—a two and a ten—and waved my hand over the ten, and let him deal me another card on the two. His own cards were a seven and a six, and if I held outright, I would get closer to twenty-one than he was and win this round. "But the money I work for has nothing to do with him."

"You're right," Gunner said, and he studied the pair of cards before him, trying to decide if he was going to take the chance. He wasn't a pro at Blackjack, and lost more often than he won. But he liked playing, anyway.

Most of the time, gambling was about pissing away money. Now and then, though, we hit it big, and then the win was so big that it covered all the losses. I'd done the math on it. The stats were sound. I saw gambling as a business investment.

My dad didn't see it that way. And the rest of the world didn't seem to see it that way, either.

"How's Maddison doing?" I asked Gunner, changing the topic away from my dad and my money. "You're still with her?"

"Yeah, of course," Gunner said. "Looks like it's getting serious."

"Really?" I asked. "I thought you said it was just a fling."

He shrugged. "I told myself I'd keep doing it until the first real flaw popped up, and I couldn't see a reason we should move forward. But that hasn't happened yet, and we're going on a year now. And if it works, it works, right?"

"Has it really been that long?" Aaron asked from my other side. He wasn't playing with us. He always said his life was complicated enough without leaving matters to chance. To each their own.

I won the round and scraped the chips toward me, grinning. I put down another stack, and the dealer dealt a fresh hand. A three and an eight landed in front of me. I nodded at the dealer after he had a six and a queen.

Gunner whistled through his teeth. "I wouldn't push that one. He's on eighteen. You can't get closer than that."

"Always worth the risk," I said and let him deal me another. I got a king, which meant I had lost no matter which way the dealer's cards went.

I scowled and pushed the stack of money toward him.

"Again," I said.

Aaron and Gunner only glanced at each other, but they knew me well enough to know that I wasn't going to listen to them if they told me to stop. I knew my limits, and I knew what my bank balance was. I knew when it was time to draw the line.

"So, how are you and Ava doing?" Aaron asked.

I shrugged. "We're doing fine. What's there to say?"

"You're living together. That's gotta count for something. What's she like to live with?"

"She's actually really great to live with," I said. "She's easygoing, doesn't take up a ton of space, and she didn't march in there and make demands right away about wanting to change anything. She makes me coffee in the morning. A model roommate. And she works fucking late, even when she's home. She has a work ethic like nothing else. I think I'm going to ask her to study for the bar exam again."

"Why?" Gunner asked.

"Because she has a hell of a mind on her, and with her knowledge of the law, she'll be a killer lawyer. It's what she wants. She just struggles with the bar, but I think I can help her with that."

Aaron and Gunner exchanged glances again.

"I'm getting sick of you guys and your meaningful glances," I snapped. "It's like you guys are my parents, having this silent conversation about how well I'm doing. What the fuck is up with that?"

"We're not giving each other meaningful glances," Aaron said with a shrug. "It just sounds to me like this arrangement you have with Ava is turning into something more than just an arrangement."

"What do you mean?" I asked.

"You talk about her like she's everything," Gunner said. "How smart she is, her future...and you want to get involved in it."

I snorted. "Not like *that*. I just see her potential, and I know she deserves more."

"You sound like you might be in love with her," Aaron said matter-of-factly.

"No, way," I said.

"Sounds like it to me," Gunner said and leaned back, stretching his back until it popped. "You're pussy whipped, man. Are you guys sleeping together?"

I thought about how Ava had kissed me, the way her body fit against mine perfectly.

And how amazing it had been having her in my bed and waking up next to her the following morning. Not just as a one-night stand I needed to get rid of, but as someone I knew, someone I'd wanted to have breakfast with.

Fuck if I was going to admit that to the guys, though. They didn't need to know how I felt about Ava. I didn't want to put it into words.

If I did, it would mean that I admitted to the fact that I was slowly falling in love with her. That was just looking for trouble.

The reason I'd told her about Adele, about how I acted, and that it wasn't normal for me to be the way I was around her, was so that she understood what was going on when the time came that we had to go our separate ways.

Because eventually, that was going to happen. And the last thing I wanted was for her to get hurt. Ava was a great person, and as time had crawled on and I'd gotten to know her better, the last thing I wanted to do was be the reason she cried.

I also wasn't going to allow myself to get hurt, though. The only option for this to end the right way was to, in fact, end it.

But that wasn't happening just yet. We still had some time left. We had a whole bunch of months left ahead of us.

I just had to keep the bigger picture in mind, and remind myself that this wasn't a long-term arrangement. Eventually, she would leave, I would be a partner in my law firm, and we would have exactly what we wanted.

All that remained was for me to remember exactly what it was that I wanted, and not let myself get distracted by how good everything felt right now.

Shit like this didn't last. No matter how good it felt.

I didn't have to get burned a second time to know that.

13

Ava

I searched for a Cajun chicken spice recipe and found one that would work. I'd already butterflied the chicken breasts, and vegetables were roasting in the oven.

While I mixed the different spices together for the rub, I listened to music on my phone. I hummed along while I rubbed the chicken on both sides. I placed them in a dish, and added thick slices of cream cheese on each. I completed the dish by adding strips of red and yellow peppers on top of the cheese, and put it in the second oven as soon as it was preheated to the right temperature.

I heard the heavy front door open, and my stomach erupted in butterflies.

"Ava?" Noah called out. "It smells incredible in here." He found me in the kitchen. "What are you doing?"

"I'm cooking us dinner," I said and smiled.

"What are you making?"

"Cajun chicken, rice, and veggies. Is that okay?" I hadn't even asked if Noah had any food allergies.

"That sounds amazing," he said.

"Then food will be ready in half an hour. I just need the chicken to cook. But I have this." I produced a plate with Italian Sub pinwheels that I'd made out of wraps: lettuce, tomato, salami, and cream cheese. I'd sliced the wraps into thick rounds and pinned them down with toothpicks so they wouldn't unravel. "Starters."

"Wow," Noah said, and took one. He popped it into his mouth, pulling the toothpick back out.

He chewed a few times, before he groaned.

"This is amazing. Did you make these?"

I nodded.

"I didn't realize you were so adept in the kitchen."

I shrugged. "My dad and I used to cook together all the time."

Talking about him made a pang shoot through my chest. We had such a great relationship. It was so hard to learn what he'd done to us after he'd died. I'd always thought I knew him, but he'd been a completely different person.

"I'm sorry," Noah said softly, seeing the shift in my mood.

I shook it off.

"It's fine," I said brightly. "You can have more if you want."

Noah eagerly took another.

"What can I do to help?" he asked.

"You can open a bottle of wine," I suggested.

"I'm on it." Noah moved around the kitchen, and I checked on the vegetables roasting in the oven.

After our night together, and how Noah acted toward me, I'd wanted to surprise him with something special. I didn't want to buy him anything—that could be weird, plus I didn't know what he liked, and he probably didn't need anything, anyway. I also didn't want to keep throwing myself at him. As wonderful as it was to sleep with him, it was looking for trouble. Besides, I wanted to get to know him better. I wanted to spend time with him where we could talk.

A dinner had seemed like the perfect solution.

Noah opened the bottle of wine and poured it into a decanter. While it breathed on the counter, he took out plates and cutlery, and set the dining room table.

When the food was ready, we each made up a plate, and walked to the dining room. We sat down, and Noah lifted his glass to me.

"What are we drinking to?" I asked.

"To being unlikely friends through all of this," I said.

Noah smirked at me. "Friends? Well, I guess we are. At the very least." He winked at me, and my heart skipped a beat.

We clinked our glasses together and took a sip.

While we ate, Noah talked about his day at the office. I loved hearing him talk, and I enjoyed it when he told me what it was like in court.

"I'm telling you, that judge hates me," Noah said, laughing. "I think it's because she's a woman."

"That's totally sexist to say," I laughed.

"Let me rephrase. I think it's because I slept with her."

I burst out laughing, surprised at the admission.

"It was a long time ago, before I was a lawyer and she was a judge. We were just two stupid people, doing stupid things. But women always hold on to stuff like that. No offense."

"None taken," I said and took a sip of my wine. A part of me was offended at the remark, even though I'd said I wasn't. Because something like sleeping with someone *was* a big deal, and holding onto it was normal. It was the reason I'd been so pissed at Noah at first, because he hadn't called me back that time after our first night.

I understood him better now, though. And it wasn't like I'd been looking for something more than a good night to help me forget either. It was just that he hadn't called me back. The fact that I needed men in my life I could trust for a change. Men who were solid, stable, who showed me what I was in for and didn't waver in that.

I was in way over my head with Noah, if that was what I wanted. He was the furthest thing from stable.

"You haven't said anything about your day," Noah said after we'd talked a while more.

"There isn't much to tell. I don't have exciting court stories, I have boring stories about cases and loopholes and figuring out ways around them. Sometimes, I envy that you can go to court."

"You should take the bar exam again, Ava," Noah said. "I'm serious. You know more about the law than all of us lawyers at SFR together. You'll wipe the floor with any opponents when you get to court with what you know."

I shrugged. "I just freeze up in tests and exams, and then everything I know goes out the window, and I stare at the piece of paper like an idiot who knows nothing." I covered my face with my hands. My cheeks burned with the wine in my blood. "I just don't think it's in the stars for me."

Noah snorted. "That sounds like a bullshit excuse to me."

"What?" I asked, blinking at him in surprise. "Did you just say it's a bullshit excuse?"

"If it's what you want, you'll make it happen," Noah said.

I was irritated. "So, do you think me failing the test twice is also an excuse?"

"No. But saying you're not supposed to be a lawyer because of a stupid test is an excuse. So, you freeze up. So, tests are fucking hard.

So, what? It's what you want, isn't it? You've done crazy stuff to get what you want in every other aspect of your life."

That was true. Being married to Noah for the sake of saving my home and taking care of my mom was a perfect example of that.

"I'm just scared I'll fail again," I admitted. "I hate being a failure. I've always been so good at everything, always getting good grades at school. Failing is a hard pill to swallow."

"Let me help you," Noah said. "I passed it the first time because I approached it the right way."

I cocked my head and considered it.

"Okay," I said slowly. "But I'm only taking it one more time. Then, if I still don't pass, I'll just have to resign myself to being a paralegal forever."

"You can do it," Noah said. His determination was sweet.

And attractive.

But damn it, everything he did was attractive.

"So..." Noah said, "...I have a proposition for you."

"Yeah?"

He nodded. "My family has an annual formal lunch at a fancy hotel. Would you like to come with me?"

"As your date?" I asked.

Noah grinned. "Yeah. As my date. Since you already happen to be my wife."

I smiled, but a thought occurred to me.

"You're going to introduce me to your family."

"Sure," Noah said. "It's not like they don't know about you. My dad would have told them, anyway. And they're really nice. Besides, I think it could be fun. Something that isn't work related. What do you say?"

Was this a good idea? Being Noah's date gave me shivers. I liked the idea that he considered me as more than just a friend, although that was what we'd toasted to. But was I ready to meet his family? To be introduced as his wife? It was a tall order.

Why did he want that from me? What was happening here?

"Come on, it will be fun," Noah said and grinned again, turning on the charm. "My family fight over something different every year, it will be entertaining. Like the Gladiators in ancient Rome."

"Did you just compare your family to a bloodbath for the sake of entertainment?" I asked.

Noah laughed. "Yeah, I did. Doesn't that make you curious?" He raised his eyebrows at me, and I laughed.

"When is it?"

"Next weekend."

"Okay," I said and laughed again. "Fine. Let's do it. Let's be entertained."

Noah laughed and nodded, pleased that I'd agreed. And maybe he was right—it *could* be fun. I barely got out to do anything outside of work these days. If I wasn't working myself to death, or sleeping a few hours to catch up, I was either visiting my mom or unpacking my drama to Paige. A change of scenery would be a good idea.

And the thought that Noah wanted me on his arm as his date made me weak in the knees, and I had to fight the urge to blush.

It was nice of him. A lot of things about him were nice these days.

It wasn't going to last, though. It couldn't. It was easy to get swept away by us playing house, sleeping together, going out on dates, and having romantic dinners. I just had to remember what this was all for. And that it wouldn't last forever.

But that was fine. I didn't want to spend the rest of my life with someone like Noah, anyway. At least...not the Noah I thought he was when I'd agreed to this.

Now that I got to know him, I saw a different man. And this Noah was someone I could easily spend much more time with than just a year in a fake marriage.

Don't go there, I scolded myself.

There was no need to complicate things more than they already were. We just had to keep it simple.

A simple dinner. A simple date.

A simple marriage... that would end in a simple divorce.

14

Noah

Every year, my family chose the Oceanside Hotel and Resort for their family dinner. Why the fuck we had to go somewhere else when we could have a family dinner at my parents' place was beyond me, but that was what we did. If there was one thing the rich and famous, upper crust elite of Seattle clung to as if their lives depended on it, it was tradition.

And coming to the hotel, spending ridiculous amounts of money on top-tier food and alcohol, was one of the most important traditions in our family.

"How are you feeling?" I asked Ava when we got into the car together.

"Still a little sick, but it will pass. I just think I'm not handling the stress very well."

"You work too hard," I said.

She shrugged. She wouldn't back down. She worked her fingers to the bone. But I admired her work ethic so much. I admired everything about her, actually.

"So, they don't do it for anyone's birthday?" Ava asked when we drove through Seattle. She flipped down the sun visor to check her makeup in the mirror.

"You look beautiful, Ava. Stop worrying."

She glanced at me and blushed. "I'm just nervous about meeting your family."

"You already know my dad."

"And he doesn't like me, remember?"

"He doesn't dislike you. He's just pissed because of what we did."

She nodded and closed the sun visor again, sitting back in the leather seat of my car. She let out a shuddering breath, glancing out of the window as the city slid by.

My dad didn't hate Ava. He'd liked her a lot when he'd hired her, and she was a great employee. Hell, she was one of the best paralegals I'd ever seen. She would make a hell of a lawyer and I was pretty sure my dad felt the same.

He was so angry because I'd pulled one over on him. I'd found a loophole in his perfect plan to force me to do what he wanted, and there wasn't anything he could do about it.

Except promote me, which was exactly what he wasn't doing. The old man still hadn't allowed anything to change in the office, even though I'd done *exactly* as he'd asked.

"You see, it works like this," I said, getting back to her question to keep the conversation flowing. I wanted to distract her from her nerves. "If they plan this event close to someone's birthday, it will be a combination, and they'll offer up an opportunity to go all out again."

Ava's lips curved into a smile, and her eyes danced with laughter. "So, they're doing this as far away from any birthday as they can so they can celebrate again when it comes down to it?"

"That's exactly it," I said with a chuckle. "If we can't splurge as much money as possible for every event imaginable...what's the point?"

Ava giggled and shook her head, her dark hair flipping over her shoulder. "I don't understand that way of life at all. I'm still trying to get used to the idea that I don't have all that debt anymore, let alone spending money so extravagantly."

I shrugged. We came from two different walks of life.

When we stopped at the resort, a valet took the car. I took Ava's hand and pressed it to my lips.

"It's going to be fine," I said.

She nodded, but her smile had slipped away, and she pursed her lips.

We walked into the resort together.

A hostess took us through the luxurious restaurant, and I held Ava tightly by my side as we weaved through the tables. I spotted our family at the other side of the restaurant, at a long table situated by the large windows that overlooked the water.

My dad stood when we arrived and shook my hand. He held out his hand to Ava, too.

"Glad you two could make it," he said.

"Thank you for the invitation," Ava said politely.

We went through the process of introducing Ava to my family. My mom, Paula, was gracious toward Ava. She greeted her with a warm smile.

"I was hoping I would get to meet you," she said. "You've been a part of the family for too long for Noah to keep hiding you away."

Ava blushed. "We've been very busy at the office."

"Oh, I know how that goes, dear. I never see Archie, and I live with the man." She smiled at my dad, who only shook his head.

"Do you see a lot of her, Noah?" Celine asked.

"This is my sister, Celine," I said to Ava.

Celine looked Ava up and down, her eyes much more judgmental than my mom's had been. I knew Ava had been the main topic of discussion in my home since the day I'd gotten married.

"I'd welcome you to the family, but you're here whether I do or not." She smiled curtly, turned her back on Ava, and walked back to her seat.

Ava looked shocked.

"Don't mind her, she's full of shit," I murmured in her ear.

Ava nodded slightly.

I introduced her to a few aunts and uncles, who I only saw a few times a year. The conversation was polite, and we kept it short—there wasn't that much to say, anyway.

Finally, we sat down.

"Shall we get started?" I asked my mom.

"Not yet. We're waiting for one more guest," she said.

I frowned and glanced around. "Who? We're all here, aren't we?"

Just as I said it, the hostess brought another member of our party to the table.

My heart stopped and my blood ran cold.

"Ah, Adele, here you are!" my mom cried out and jumped up to hug her. "I'm so, so glad you could join us."

"What is she doing here?" I asked in a low voice.

"Mom invited her," Celine said nonchalantly. "She's always been like part of the family, you know."

"She gave up that right a long time ago," I growled.

"Maybe when it comes to you, but we see her now and then." Celine took a sip from her wine glass. "Go easy on her. She's just been through a messy divorce."

I snorted. "I'm willing to bet on what tore that relationship apart." Celine only glared at me.

"What's going on?" Ava asked. She'd picked up on the tension.

"It's nothing," I said curtly.

Adele walked around the table after greeting my parents, and hugged my sister as if she was a long lost friend. I watched her. She looked exactly the same as she had years ago, when I'd dumped her for sleeping with someone else.

Her copper hair had been brushed out until it flowed like silk, thick and shiny on her shoulders. Her skin was flawless, and she wore a dress that I knew would have cost a small fortune.

The only thing more important to Adele than getting what she wanted, was her image. I bristled as I watched her, feeling sick to my stomach. It had been a decade since I'd seen her last, but the pain of what she'd done to me came right back.

Finally, she turned to me.

"Hi, Noah. It's nice to see you again."

"I wish I could say the same," I said.

"Noah," mom said sharply.

I shook my head. "This is Ava, my wife."

Adele looked at Ava down her nose for a long moment, sizing her up. She raised her eyebrows and pursed her lips. Yeah, she found Ava lacking.

"Congratulations," she finally said. "I hope you have what it takes to deal with him more than I did." She offered a tight smile before she turned away and took her seat.

I shook my head and tried to swallow my emotions. My head spun as my blood rushed to my ears.

"Are you okay?" Ava asked softly.

"Perfectly fine," I lied.

She put her hand on my arm, trying to reassure me. I pulled my arm away.

I wasn't trying to be a dick—really. But it felt like my world was caving in. My skin prickled with anger I was just barely able to contain. I tugged at my collar, trying to keep it together. I had to put on a good face for the party. We had to get through five main courses and mediocre conversation. I had to smile and gasp in all the right places and look like I actually wanted to fucking be here.

Which I didn't. Not now that they'd invited the bitch from hell.

Everything I'd worked so hard to forget over the past decade came rushing back at me as if it had happened yesterday. Adele and her infidelity, giving herself to someone else as if I meant nothing. I'd worked so fucking hard to move past it, to forget, to act like it had never happened. It had worked, too. I mean, I'd been happy the past decade, right? I hadn't dated, but I'd fucked, drank and done everything I'd wanted.

It turned out that not dealing with my issues didn't work. It came back to bite me in the ass in the end.

Go fucking figure.

A server poured us wine into our glasses. I downed my glass before the server was finished filling Ava's glass and held it out for another round. Ava only watched me without saying anything.

"You know what? Fuck this shit." I stood, and the table fell silent, everyone staring at me. "We're leaving."

"Sit down, Noah," Dad said.

"No, Dad," I said and turned to Ava. "Let's get out of here."

She stood. I didn't know if she wanted to get out of here as quickly as she could, too. I was just glad she was coming with me.

"Thank you for having me," she said politely.

I took her hand and led her away, not caring that the table erupted in a bout of gossip, that they all thought I was pathetic or a piece of shit or unable to handle my emotions. I didn't fucking care. All I cared about was getting away from everyone who forced me into doing things I hated.

"What's going on, Noah?" Ava asked when we left the resort in my car.

"I just had to get away from them and all their pretenses. What about something more fun?"

"Okay," she said, still unsure. "You're sure you're okay?"

"Now that I'm away from the bunch of stiffs, you bet."

I floored it, flying through the streets. I knew exactly where we were going.

When we stopped in front of the casino, Ava frowned.

"What are we doing here?"

"We're having fun," I said.

She glanced at me. "I don't know if gambling is my idea of fun. And I don't feel very well…"

"That's just because you haven't done it with me, sweetheart. We won't stay long. I just want to blow off some steam." I got out of the car. Ava followed me, her heels clicking on the tarmac as we crossed the parking lot. When we stepped into the casino, the sounds were familiar, welcoming me home.

I was a platinum card holder at the casino, which meant I could drink as much as I wanted for free. I ordered a whiskey from the closest server, walking around in a black waistcoat.

"What do you want?" I asked Ava.

She shook her head. "Nothing for me."

I shrugged, and we walked to a Blackjack table. Ava looked uncomfortable when she sat down. She would relax if she drank something, but it was her call. The last thing I wanted to do was to force her into something she didn't like. I had more than enough experience with what that felt like with my family, and I didn't wish that shit on anyone.

When my whiskey arrived, I threw it back and promptly asked for another.

The dealer put down a seven and a nine for me.

"Oh," I said. "We're starting this off on a shaky foot, huh?"

The dealer didn't respond. He only put down a queen and an eight for himself.

"Fuck." He was so close to twenty-one, I had to hit it on the head if I wanted to win this round.

"Fold," I said.

Half my bet went back to the stack and half went to the dealer.

"Hit me again," I said. I glanced at Ava, who watched the cards with a clenched jaw. Her eyes were large, and she looked unsure of herself.

The dealer put down a six and a four.

"That's more like it. Again." I glanced at Ava. "Do you know how the game works?"

She nodded tightly.

"Come on, Ava. Relax."

She only glanced at me and didn't relax at all. Her tension frustrated me. What was her issue?

When the dealer put down another card, it was a nine. He had ten and a three. When he drew his card, it was a jack.

I pumped a fist into the air and rubbed my hands together when the dealer pushed a stack of chips toward me.

For a while, the cards were in my favor and my stack of chips grew bigger and bigger. Ava didn't enjoy herself one bit. But the whiskey was free-flowing. I kept winning, and between getting drunk and riding on the high of winning, I was having a blast.

"Can we go, soon?" Ava asked. "I feel so sick."

"One more hand," I said. "Then we'll go."

She nodded, and I told the dealer to hit me again, pushing my chips into the center of the table.

Ava gasped. "That's everything you just won."

"Double or nothing, honey, that's what I always say. When I win this one, I'll take us away on a holiday."

"It's stupid to do that," Ava scolded. "Come on, why don't we just go?"

"No way. Lady luck is smiling down on me, babe. I'm not going anywhere until I get what I want."

"And what's that?"

"To win!" I cried out.

Ava shook her head. "It always starts like this. Do you know where it ends?"

"In a very good place," I said with a grin.

Ava rolled her eyes and shook her head. But I nodded at the dealer. It was time to make it rain.

He dealt with a seven and a four. When he put down his own cards, he had a ten and a Jack.

"Fuck!" I cried out, staring at his cards.

"Noah..." Ava said softly.

I groaned and shook my head. "We can't go now."

"Did you just lose it all?" she asked.

I shook my head. "It doesn't matter. There's a lot more where that came from."

She shook her head and stood. "You played your hand. We're leaving, now."

"I can win it back," I said.

"I'm not waiting here for you to do that. I know how this ends, Noah, and it's not pretty." She turned around and walked away.

"Damn it, Ava," I said and hopped off my chair, running after her. "You don't need to leave. It's not such a big deal."

"I just want to go home," she said.

Her eyes shimmered with tears when she looked at me, but she blinked again, and they were gone. The casino spun slowly around me, and I wasn't sure if it had been just the alcohol or if she'd really just cried because I'd lost a metric fuck ton of money.

"Okay," I finally said. "Let's go."

She nodded, and we walked out of the casino. The sun had already started to set, and the world was painted with grays and blues, the colors of the night.

I'd been gambling for hours. A pang of guilt shot into my chest—she felt sick, and she'd been waiting patiently for me even though she hadn't been having a good time. I shoved the guilt away—I could do what I wanted, and I hadn't held a gun to her head, forcing her to sit here with me.

I wouldn't allow myself to feel something. I'd switched myself off, and the oblivion was a glorious break from the storm that had appeared when I'd seen Adele.

"Give me the keys," Ava ordered.

"Why?"

"Because you're drunk and you're not driving like that."

"I'm fine," I said.

"Damn it, Noah. You're like a child! I'm not playing this game with you. Give me the keys, or I'll find my own way home."

"I guess that's what you'll have to do, then. Because I'm not letting you drive my car. You don't get to tell me what to do. You don't own me."

Where were the words coming from? I didn't mean to be such an asshole to Ava. But God, she was trying to control me, to tell me who to be and what to do, and I wasn't having any of it. I refused to listen to anyone who wanted me to be different from exactly who I was.

"Fine," Ava said, her eyes narrowed. "I guess I'll see you at home."

"I guess so," I said and climbed into my car.

She turned and walked away from the car. A part of me screamed at me that I should go after her and get her back. But that little voice—the voice of reason—drowned in alcohol and all I could think about was how Adele had asked me to change every day and give things up to be a better man, only for her to find her way into another man's bed.

This whole relationship with Ava was a fucking sham, anyway. I didn't have to do what she asked of me. I wasn't in this to gain her trust, keep her happy, or build a life with her. I was in it to get what I wanted.

Which I hadn't gotten, anyway.

I'd been a fool to think for even just a second that I could be happy with her. Being in a relationship just wasn't for me, and no matter how good something looked on the surface, it always turned out the same.

I was meant to be alone.

I put the car in gear and floored it, speeding down the road. I struggled to see straight—everything blurred together. When I took a corner too fast, I overshot, and my tire hit the curb so hard, I felt it right to my very core. That was a flat tire. A moment later, I felt it, and pulled over.

Just as I did, the sirens of a cop car sounded and pulled up behind me.

I groaned. This was going to be just *great*.

15

Ava

Noah spent the night in jail for drinking and driving, and the damage he'd done to his car when he'd hit a curb was more than just replacing a tire. He'd bent the axle, hitting the curb with enough speed that his car needed serious work.

Needless to say, his dad was furious with him. I didn't think I'd ever heard anyone shout so loudly in his office. Archie's fight with Noah had been loud enough that the entire floor could hear it. I wouldn't have been surprised if the entire building had heard it.

He'd pulled some strings and managed to get the charges dropped, of course. Noah had everyone in his pocket—he had contacts everywhere, and despite the fact that he could be a real dick, they loved him.

Well, they weren't married to him. Maybe that was why they were on his side.

"It's not that I'm *not* on his side," I said to Paige when we met during our lunch hour at a café halfway between our two offices. "I just can't deal with this. I have too much on my plate already, with work and with the bar exams coming up."

"Everyone makes mistakes, Ava," Paige said carefully, poking around in the Cobb salad she'd ordered.

"I know that. It would have been okay if it was just drinking and driving, but it's more than that. I can't do this all again."

"You're talking about the gambling," Paige said.

I nodded and cut a piece of chicken before popping it into my mouth. I'd ordered grilled chicken and vegetables so that I could last through the night—I would be pulling an all-nighter studying for the exam tomorrow. But the food turned to sand in my mouth and I felt sick to my stomach when I ate anything.

I was beyond stressed.

"It doesn't have to be the same as it was with your dad," Paige said. "You didn't know about what your dad was up to. You only found out about all the debt before he passed away. With Noah, at least, you know exactly where you stand."

"That's the thing...I don't. For a while, I thought we were going to figure it out. He was so kind and attentive and sweet and really made an effort with me. It was like we were really dating. Or married, or whatever. But now, he seems set on pushing me away. It's like a switch flipped and I have no idea what happened or what's going on. With the gambling on top of it all...I can't do it."

Paige didn't say anything. She ate her salad, and the silence stretched out between us.

I didn't blame her for not knowing what to say. I was at as much of a loss as she was.

"We still have almost seven more months to do this thing before our marriage ends," I said dully. "I'm going to have to stick it out. I don't know how I'm going to do it, though. It feels like a breakup, although nothing like that has happened and we still live in the same house."

"Maybe you should just talk to him," Paige offered. "I know it's tough, and you guys barely know each other. You jumped into this so quickly. But if things were going as well as you say they were, surely you can talk to him and find out what's going on, right?"

"Maybe you're right," I said. "But I know I'm not going to talk to him about it until I take the bar exams. I'm losing my mind stressing over this stupid exam, and I can't afford any distractions right now. Things are tough enough at home as it is."

Paige nodded. "You still have time with Noah. Focus on doing this, first."

I sighed. "I wish I knew if it was going to work out in my favor for a change. But I'm too scared to get my hopes up. In fact, I'll probably fail again." I took a sip of the sparkling water I'd ordered. My stomach turned and twisted with nausea. I took another bite of chicken, but I just felt downright sick.

"Don't talk like that," Paige said, finishing her salad. She put her knife and fork together. "You're going to be just fine. You're going to make this happen. Third time's a charm, right?"

"Or it will be the third time I fail," I pointed out.

"Stop it. You can do this. It's just a bad patch, my friend. The sun will come out again, you'll see."

I nodded. I wanted to believe that everything was going to be okay. I just had to hold on and get through this one step at a time. When I got back to the office, I had a few case files to work through, and then I could focus on my books. I would get through the night with coffee and energy bars, and all of this would be over in a few days.

Nothing lasted forever, not the good, but also not the bad. I just had to keep holding onto that.

ell

When I walked into the bar exam the next morning, I felt even sicker than I had until now. My stomach twisted and turned, threatening to eject the bit of food I'd put into my body a few hours ago. I had a bottle of water with me and sipped it, hoping that it would help with the nausea.

I found my seat and took a big breath. The exam was already face down on the table.

This was it. This was where my life could change drastically...or stay exactly the same. God, I hoped that it was the former. I really needed this to work. Although, now that I was here, I was terrified that I would fail.

Why had I let Noah talk me into this?

I shook off the thought of him. I hadn't even seen him the last couple of days—I'd left before he'd woken up and gotten home long before he did. By the time he'd come home, I'd been asleep again.

Or I stayed at the office throughout the night, and barely saw him at all.

It was easier this way. I hated that we were so detached from each other, and he was so distant. But whatever he was going through, he had to go through it alone. I couldn't be there for him right now.

And it seemed he wasn't going to be there for me, either.

I forced everything away and only focused on the exam in front of me. When I could flip over the paper, I looked at the questions, and started writing.

The bar exam consisted of twelve hours of testing, split over two days. This was the first day. I'd be sitting for the multistate essay exam and the multistate performance test. Tomorrow, I would write the multistate bar exam.

And then it would all be over.

After six hours of testing, I felt like I was going to faint. I was light-headed and nauseous, and I felt shaky. When I stepped outside, my stomach twisted and turned, the nausea overwhelming me. I couldn't hold it back anymore. Bile pushed up my throat, and I hurried to a trash can. I threw up in it, retching and gagging until it was all out and my stomach was empty.

"Are you okay?" a woman who'd been at the exam with me asked.

"The stress is killing me," I said.

She nodded and handed me a tissue to wipe my mouth. I was grateful.

"It's so tough, but you've got this. Just keep pushing through and we'll make it."

I straightened out and looked at her smiling face. She was blonde with blue eyes and she looked timid, not at all like a lawyer.

"You seem to be handling it okay," I said.

"Oh, I'm a mom. We can handle stress like nothing you've ever seen." She grinned at me. "The last time I threw up like that, I was pregnant. You've got this. Good luck!" she walked away from me, and I pressed the tissue to my lips. My stomach twisted again, but I didn't throw up another time.

Pregnant?

There was no way I could be pregnant. This was stress—it had to be. Except...I'd never thrown up from stress like this before, and this wasn't my first rodeo. It was the third time I was taking this exam.

I tried to figure out when last I'd had my period. The last couple of months blurred together in my mind, and I had no idea. I couldn't even link it to an event that stood out because aside from Noah's ridiculous drunken day, I'd only ever spent time working and sleeping.

There was no way I could be pregnant, though. Noah and I had used protection every time. Except for that one time when he'd nearly forgotten, but I'd stopped him quickly, and he'd wrapped up after that.

Impossible. I wasn't pregnant.

I got into my car and drove back to the office for a half-day of work, but I couldn't shake the nausea. That only made me panic more and more about the possibility.

"Damn it," I muttered to myself and pulled over, stopping in front of a convenience store. I was going to take a stupid test so that I would know once and for all. At least that would be one less thing to worry about.

The tests were all lined up together. I grabbed two different kinds of tests and avoided making eye contact with the woman behind the counter when I paid. I didn't want to know what she was thinking. I didn't want her to ask me if I was excited or nervous, if we'd been trying. I didn't want any of this.

When I arrived at the office, I got out of my car, rode the elevator to my floor, and walked straight to the ladies' room. I went through the whole pee-on-a-stick process and waited the two minutes. All the while, I told myself I was being stupid. I was just wasting my time. There was no way I was pregnant, no way I was going to expect a child on top of everything else that seemed to go wrong in my life. I just had to go through the motions to know for a fact that it was something I could rule out, and then I could keep going.

When the time was up, I looked at the tests.

Both of them had a plus.

Both of them told me I was pregnant.

I frowned at the tests, and the world around me fell away. Blood drained from my face, and I had to grab onto the wall so that I didn't fall. I felt wobbly on my legs. My ears rang.

I couldn't be pregnant. There was no fucking way.

I wrapped both tests in toilet paper before putting them in the bin, just in case someone noticed it when they threw something away. I walked to my office in a daze. How could this be? How could so much go wrong in one person's life? What had I done to deserve this!?

When I sat down behind my desk, Belinda appeared.

"How did it go?" she asked.

"What?"

She blinked at me. "The test."

Oh. The exam.

"Fine. I don't know what the outcome will be...I guess we'll just have to see."

"I know you did great," Belinda said with a smile.

"Thanks," I said.

She frowned. "Are you okay?"

"Just stressed," I said. It wasn't a lie. Now that I'd found out I was pregnant, I was more stressed than ever.

Belinda disappeared again, and I powered up my laptop. I opened a case file. I went through the motions on autopilot.

I was pregnant with Noah's child. Oh, God. What was going to become of us after all this was over if I was having his baby? Right now, he didn't even want to see me, let alone raise a child with me, or build a life with me...

My phone rang, jerking me harshly out of the spiral of my thoughts.

Kyle's name flashed on the caller ID. The last thing I could do right now was deal with my ex.

I silenced the call, took a deep breath.

And burst into tears.

16

Noah

When I walked into the Cavaliers' headquarters, my dad was sitting at the bar. Aaron was sitting with him.

I groaned. I wanted to spend time with my best friend, but I didn't want to talk to my dad. He'd already let the whole world know what a fuck up I was when he'd screamed at me in his office. There was nothing else he could tell me that I didn't already know—I was a disappointment in his eyes, and nothing I did would change that.

Not even growing up and getting fucking married like he wanted.

Although, in his defense, it wasn't like I'd done that the right way, either. Everything I'd done had been a disappointment.

Whatever.

I walked to the bar and sat down next to Aaron. He drained his glass of whiskey and set it down.

"Timing is shit, man," he said apologetically. "I have to go."

"Already?"

He nodded. "Ben and I are having a boys' night. Can't be late."

I wanted to argue, but I knew that Ben would win out no matter what my argument was. Aaron had priorities, and he stuck to them.

"I'll see you later," he said, clapping me on the back.

I sighed when he walked away, and it was just me and my dad at the bar together. Later, some of the other Cavaliers would join us—I expected Landon and his son Brad to show up once they finished at the office, and later, Gunner and the rest would follow, too. But for now, it was just the two of us.

"You're here early," I said to my dad. He usually stayed in the office until most of the others had left, doing what needed to be done to earn his keep.

He shrugged. "Sometimes those four walls can drive you crazy."

I nodded. "I guess they can."

Dad studied me, and I braced myself. When the tongue-lashing didn't come, I rolled my eyes.

"Go on, say what you need to say," I said. "Tell me how I'm fucking up my life."

"That's not what I was going to say," Dad said.

I glanced at him, and when the whiskey I'd ordered arrived, I took a sip.

"Then what?" I asked.

"What's going on with you?" Dad asked. "You're usually full of shit, but you've hit a new level."

"There are levels to how I can disappoint you?" I snapped.

Dad rolled his eyes. "Don't be a dick, Noah. I'm trying to talk to you. Something is going on. I'm not trying to lecture you, I'm trying to figure you out."

I sighed heavily. "Thanks."

"It's Adele, isn't it?"

I glared at him. "Why do you ask?"

"Because your mother invited her to the event, and you've been spiraling even more since then."

I bristled. I hated talking about Adele, and I hated that my dad had figured out that was what bugged me.

"I'll get over it," I growled.

"Not if drinking away your sorrows is how you're planning on doing it," Dad pointed out. "Alcohol doesn't fix anything."

"Neither does milk."

He snorted a laugh. "No, you're right. What I'm trying to say is that you need to face the facts and deal with them instead of running away. You've been running for a decade."

"Damn it, Dad, I'm just about sick of hearing how I'm doing everything wrong. Can't you give me a break?"

"Give yourself a break," Dad clapped back.

I glared at him.

"For the record, I didn't think it was right of your mother to invite Adele. Not after everything that woman put you through. But Paula still seems to think you two belong together, no matter how far we are down the line."

"You don't agree?" I asked.

"Of course, not. She's a two-faced bitch, only here for the money, and she's not going to treat you right. You'll be miserable with her."

I couldn't believe what I was hearing. I'd never thought my dad would be on my side.

"Ava is good for you," Dad added in a gentler tone. "I know you only married her to get back at me, but the more I get to know her.. .let's just say you've made far worse mistakes."

"Yeah? Well, it's not going to last," I said. "It's not like we planned for this to work in the long run."

"I suspected as much. But for a while there, watching you two interact at the office...I thought you might figure it out."

I shook my head. There had been a time when I'd thought we could figure it out, too. I'd wanted it so fucking badly. But that ship had sailed.

"I can't do it," I said.

"Why not?"

"I can't afford to do this all again. I can't be with her, get attached, invest everything I have—"

"Only for it to fail?" Dad asked, finishing my sentence for me.

I didn't want to nod and agree. I didn't want to admit that my dad had hit the nail on the head. But somehow, he'd figured shit out about me I'd thought I'd kept hidden really well.

"How do you know?" I asked.

"Noah, you're my son. I work with you. I see you every day. Do you think I don't know you?"

"You gave me a ridiculous ultimatum to make partner," I pointed out.

"Yeah...I didn't think you were going to pay someone to marry you, though."

I paled. "You know about that?"

Dad grinned. "Well, no. I suspected it, but you now just confirmed it."

I bristled that he'd tricked it out of me, but what did it matter? My dad already knew everything about my royal screw ups. This was just another drop in the ocean.

"It's not wrong to put yourself out there again. Not everyone is like Adele."

"No, but why take the chance?" I asked. "Most women just want the money, anyway. And that's why Ava is here, too. For the money.

Even though I was the one who offered it—it's still what she's here for. She wouldn't have done it if it wasn't about the money."

My dad nodded and sipped his drink slowly. I couldn't tell what he was thinking, but that was nothing new.

"Why did you tell me to get married if you didn't think that was what I was going to do?"

"I just wanted to snap you out of your downward spiral," Dad said. "I figured if I told you to do something you were dead set against, you would meet me somewhere in the middle, and that would be enough."

I blinked at him. "So, you would have made me partner if I just stopped drinking and screwing around."

Dad shrugged, and I groaned.

"Would have been great if you'd talked to me about it."

"I tried that," Dad said. "But...the Forger men have never been great at communication."

I nodded.

"Look, you fucked up by getting married. I'm not going to deny that. But Ava seems to be different from the other women you've had in your life. Your whole setup had an expiration date, so I don't know if you can expect anything else. At least take it as proof that not everyone is like Adele. When you're free of this whole business with her, you might consider trying again for the right reasons."

Maybe my dad was right. Not everyone was like Adele—especially not Ava. But Ava was different from any other woman I'd been with. That was what I loved so much about her.

And what scared the living shit out of me? I was falling for her. Hard.

And I wasn't good enough for her. I'd realized that when I'd ended up in jail for a night, when I'd been locked up for acting like a damn fool.

Now, I couldn't look her in the eye.

It would be better when this was all over. She wasn't the girl for me—she had different values, different goals. She didn't like the way I lived my life.

And I wasn't going to change for her. I deserved to be the person I wanted to be. I deserved to make my own choices and chart my own course.

The doors to the bar opened, and a bunch of men walked in, talking and laughing.

Landon spotted us. "Getting a head start, eh?" he asked, laughing before he clapped my dad on his back and shook my head. "Don't worry, we can catch up. Right, boys?"

Brad and Gunner had been talking to each other, and they stopped their conversation and nodded.

I plastered a smile on my face, pretending that nothing was wrong. Dad was smiling, too. We'd perfected the fake smile over the years, and no one would have guessed that a moment ago, we'd had a strange heart to heart that was a first in our father-son history.

"You good?" Gunner asked when Landon and my dad got into it about football scores.

"Fine," I said. "Why?"

Gunner shrugged. "Just asking. How's Ava?"

"I don't know. Fine, I guess. She wrote her bar exam today."

"How did it go?"

I shrugged. I hadn't asked her.

Gunner shook his head. "You know, if you want to create some form of relationship, the first thing you need to do is ask her how shit's going for her after a long day, or after big deals like the bar exam."

"Is that how you and Maddison deal with it?" I asked.

Gunner nodded. "That's the point of a relationship. Talking. Getting right down to the nitty gritty with each other."

"Hmm," I said. "That doesn't sound like me."

"And that's why you're not the dating type," Gunner said with a laugh.

I clinked my glass against his, as if toasting how fucked up I was in a relationship was a good thing.

But one thing my dad had said was true—Ava and I had an expiration date on our relationship. And we weren't right for each other. We were different people with different values.

We weren't going to work in the long run.

It was better to call it quits when we said we would and be done with it. Rather than trying to make this work only to figure out eventually that we couldn't. I didn't feel like a lot of heartache, and she deserved way better, too.

I just had to get used to the idea of losing her.

After an evening of drinking, I still felt as sober as before I'd started. What the fuck was that all about? Usually, alcohol helped me drown my sorrows and get rid of any pesky thoughts that plagued me. Tonight, it didn't seem to work.

After I'd tried for a couple of hours, I left the building and called a cab. I'd learned my lesson about driving drunk. Not that I was drunk, but a breathalyzer was going to land me in jail again, and I didn't feel like another night groveling and bribing to keep my record clean. Once in a lifetime of that was enough.

I wanted to go home. I wanted to sleep. But Ava was at home, and I had no idea how I would face her.

Instead, I told the driver to take me to the office. There was always something to work on, and drowning in work was something that had worked for my dad for years. I could do that, too.

The cab pulled up in front of the building. I was about to open the door when I spotted Ava, standing on the curb. Another man stood by her. I frowned—who was this guy? He didn't look familiar. He took her hands in his and pulled her closer, and something inside me snapped.

"I changed my mind," I said to the driver, barely thinking straight. My ears burned, and I felt like breaking something. "I want to go home." I gave the driver the address, and he turned the car around. I forced myself not to look back at Ava.

This whole fucking relationship wasn't real, so why did it bother me that she was with another guy?

It was simple. I hadn't promised my heart to her when we'd gotten married, but despite our agreement, I hadn't tried to sleep with anyone else out of respect for her. And here she was, making nice with a guy who wasn't *me*.

And I was done.

17

Ava

"Ava," a deep voice said when I stepped out of the building. My head throbbed from a relentless pounding in my temples, and I felt sick. I'd taken my bar exam this morning—the second day of two—and came right back to the office to put in a full day's work.

Now, I just wanted to go home.

I stopped and turned toward the sound of my name. When the shadowy figure stepped into the light that shone through the doors I'd just exited, I recognized him immediately.

"Kyle? What are you doing here?"

"I just wanted to see you," he said.

He looked almost exactly the same as he had when we'd called it off a year and a half ago. His dark hair was a mess, but under the thick jacket he was wearing, he looked thinner, more hollowed out. I glanced up at him—I'd forgotten just how tall he was.

"How did you know where I work?" I asked.

"I looked you up. I know I shouldn't have, and I'm not a creeper, I swear. I just...you didn't answer my calls or my texts, and I really needed to see you."

I narrowed my eyes. I was exhausted. I didn't have the strength to deal with this on top of everything else.

"This is inappropriate, Kyle. I didn't answer your calls and texts for a reason."

"Just hear me out, Ava. After everything we've been through, I deserve that much."

I shook my head. "I don't owe you anything."

"Just hear me out, okay? That's all I want. I just want to say my piece, and if you still feel the way you do..."

"You'll leave me alone?"

He shook his head. "I know it's the right thing to say, but I can't just let you go. Not when I know that you're the best thing that's ever happened to me."

I groaned.

"We belong together, Ava. It took me losing you to know that. They always say you don't know what you've got until it's gone, and they're right. I know now." He took a step closer and took both my hands in his. "Give us another chance. I know what I did wrong before, and I'll change. I'll do anything you need me to, to show you how serious I am about making this work."

I stared at my hands in his before I took a step back.

"I'm sorry, Kyle. I'm not..." I took a deep breath. "I'm married."

Kyle frowned. "What?"

"I'm married," I said again. "This is never going to happen between us. It's over, and it has been for a long time."

"When did you get married?" Kyle asked, confused. "I don't...what?"

I shook my head. "Quite frankly, it's none of your business. Please, leave me alone. Don't come to my work, don't try to find out where I live. Just leave me alone, okay?" I turned my back to him and marched away purposefully. I didn't look over my shoulder to see what expression he wore on his face, though I was pretty sure he was shocked to his core. I'd just tore away the last bit of hope that had motivated him to find me in the first place.

But I was with Noah. We might not have gotten married because we loved each other, but that didn't mean that we weren't married. That meant something to me.

I was carrying his child now, too. I wanted things to work with Noah. It had started out as being about the money, but it wasn't about that anymore. I'd fallen in love with Noah, and I wanted to be with him. I wanted this family with him.

I got into my car and drove home. I hoped he was there and awake. I needed to talk to him, to tell him how I felt. I had to tell him about the baby. Maybe that would change things for him. If he tried from his side, I would try from mine. We could work around the gambling and the drinking as long as I knew what was going on, right? And we could make this work.

When I arrived at the apartment, music blasted loudly from inside. I pushed open the door. Noah stood by the wet bar, pouring himself a glass of whiskey. He didn't just pour two or three fingers; he poured it all the way to the top.

I walked to the entertainment unit in the living room and turned down the music.

"Noah," I said. "Can we talk?"

"What do you want to talk about?" he asked coldly.

My stomach clenched with nerves. I swallowed hard and walked to him.

"I want to talk about us."

"Really?" Noah asked and offered me a twisted smile that looked a lot more like a sneer. "I didn't realize there was still an 'us'."

I frowned. "What are you talking about?"

"Does it matter what I'm talking about?" Noah asked.

I glanced at the drink in his hand. "Are you drunk?"

He laughed bitterly. "If you're here to tell me I'm not supposed to be, I'll tell you to fuck off."

"I wasn't going to say that," I said, raising my eyebrows. "And you have no right to talk to me that way."

"Ha!" Noah said, forcing a laugh. "Let's talk about my right, shall we?" He walked around the bar to the middle of the living room. He swayed slightly on his feet.

"Maybe we shouldn't talk right now," I said. I couldn't talk to him about this when he was drunk. I had no idea what his mood was about. Maybe he'd fought with his father again.

"No, I have nothing better to do. Let's talk," he said. He sipped his whiskey, looking me dead in the eye.

"Okay, well, I just wanted to—"

"Talk about us," he said. "You already said that. Are you going to stand there and try to convince me that you're not fucking someone else?"

"What!?" I cried out.

"Did you think you could get that one by me?"

"There was nothing to get by you. I'm not sleeping with anyone."

Noah shook his head and gulped down his drink. "I'm not going to go through this again. You women are all the same. You think you can lie to me, and I'll fall for it every single time. I'm not going to stand for it."

I shook my head. He wasn't making any sense. What could have happened to make him think—

"Are you talking about Kyle?"

"So, he has a name," Noah sneered, and dropped himself onto the leather couch. His drink spilled onto his shirt, and he wiped it away with his hand.

"He's my ex," I said.

"That just makes it so much worse."

I shook my head. "He came to the office to see me because I've been ignoring him. I told him we're married. He'll leave me alone, now."

"I don't care," Noah said. He sounded tired, suddenly. "I don't care about any of it anymore."

"Noah…"

"Get out," he said.

His words hit me like a physical punch in the gut. "What?"

"I said get out! I don't want you here anymore. We're not doing this. I'm not going to be anchored to a woman who doesn't give a shit about me."

"You can't do this," I said hotly. "You're drunk, you're emotional, and you're *not* kicking me out of the house just because you think something's going on that you have no proof of."

Noah glared at me. "Get. Out."

"I'm pregnant," I said.

He stared at me, blinking. He said nothing.

"With *your* child," I added, in case he might have thought it was someone else's. Just the idea that I was cheating made me feel sick. Or maybe it was the baby—I didn't know anymore.

Noah still didn't answer me.

"Have you gone deaf?" I asked. "I'm pregnant, Noah. We're going to have a baby."

"Are you saying that to stay?" he asked.

I gasped. "I'm saying it because it's true. We're going to have a baby, you and me, and we have to work this out. For the baby's sake, and for ours. We're going to—"

"*We* are not going to do anything," Noah said coldly. He stood, and this time he seemed to be firm on his feet. He swallowed down the last of his whiskey. "*You* might have to go through it, but I'm not going to be there. We're not doing this anymore. I want a divorce."

I stared at him. My stomach dropped to my shoes. I couldn't believe Noah was kicking me out. I couldn't believe he was calling it off.

"Can't we just talk about this?" I asked.

"What's there to talk about? I was a fool getting into this at all. You got everything you wanted, you laid down the rules, and you lived the high life. But what about me? I got nothing out of this. *Nothing!*"

"You didn't want to lay down any rules!" I cried out. "And it's not my fault you didn't get your promotion the way you wanted. I kept my end of the deal all the way through."

"You're right, I didn't make any rules."

"And we broke them, anyway," I added. My chest was on fire like I had a bad case of heartburn. I pressed my hand against my chest and forced myself to breathe evenly. This wasn't how I'd pictured this conversation going at all.

"And now, I'm going to break another rule," Noah said in an even voice. "We're not waiting until the year is up before I get rid of you. I'll talk to my lawyer tomorrow and serve you the papers."

I gasped. "You're kicking me out?"

"It's not like you don't have a home to go to," he said. "I made sure of that when I paid your mortgage and took care of your debt."

He wasn't wrong. I could go back home to my mom. But that wasn't what this was about. I wanted to work things out with Noah. I wanted to be with him.

"Don't end this now, Noah," I said in a thin voice. "I'm in love with you."

He looked at me with an expressionless mask before he turned around and walked away.

A moment later, his bedroom door slammed shut, and I was left in the wake of his destruction.

18

Noah

"Is there a reason why we're getting wasted in the middle of the day or are you just being ironic?" Gunner asked.

"What does that even mean?" I asked, lying on the bar counter.

We weren't at the Cavaliers' headquarters where we usually drank. We sat in a seedy pub on the other side of Seattle.

"What happened?" Aaron asked.

"I'm single and free to do whatever I want, and what I want is to get rip-roaring drunk with my friends without old men looking over my shoulder and judging me all the time," I said. "Is that too much to ask?"

Aaron and Gunner glanced at each other.

"I don't understand what you're playing at, getting rid of her so quickly," Aaron said.

I shook my head. "I didn't ask you here because you understand, man. I just want to drink."

"Do you really want to do this?" Gunner asked. "You know, once it's done, it's done."

I scowled. "Do you think I don't know that? I'm not fucking stupid. I understand how divorce works."

Gunner shook his head and took a sip of his beer.

"I don't get you guys," I said. "This whole time, you've been telling me how stupid I was to get married to her. Now you're telling me I'm doing the wrong thing by getting rid of her?"

"That was before," Gunner said.

"Before what?"

"Before you obviously fell in love with her," Aaron said outright.

I glared at him. "I'm not in love with her."

"Yeah, I cry bullshit," Gunner said and leaned on the bar. "Since the day she walked into your life, things have started to change. You've changed."

I frowned. "It shouldn't take long before I'm back to my old self. Don't worry."

My friends both shook their heads again, but I didn't want to hear it. My mind was made up. I didn't need this bullshit in my life. It had taken so long to get over what Adele had done to me, and I wasn't ready for another one of those trips. Luckily, this time, it was pretty damn simple. Because I didn't care about Ava the way I'd cared about Adele. We'd planned to end things, anyway. It was just a matter of pushing up the due date.

"She's pregnant," I said before I sipped my beer again.

Gunner and Aaron both frowned at me.

"What?"

"You heard me," I said. "She's having a baby."

"Yours?" Aaron looked concerned.

"Who the fuck knows?" I asked. After a while of my friends still staring at me, I sighed and added, "Yeah, probably."

"And you're just going to walk away from her?" Aaron asked, his alarm growing.

I threw my hands in the air. "What the hell am I supposed to do? I don't even know if it's fucking real. Maybe she just said it to stay in my life or something. God, you know what women can be like."

"Do you really think she would have lied to you about something like that?" Gunner asked.

I shook my head. I didn't for a second think that Ava would lie to me. I just didn't want to think about what it would mean if she was having my baby. I couldn't do this damn life, I couldn't think about a long-term relationship, I couldn't think about having a baby. How the fuck was I supposed to man up and be a father, a husband, when all I knew how to be was an arrogant jerk who drank too much?

"We both knew this was going to end," I finally said. "It's just ending quicker than it should have. Come on, Aaron, you know what I'm talking about, right? It's not like I'm not going to help her out financially, but I can't be a part of the picture the way she thinks I should be."

Aaron shook his head. "Look, man, I don't know what you're all about. I know you like to party and shit, but most of it is just because you're running away from real life. That stuff isn't important. The thing is...I would never change a thing when it comes to Ben. Sure, it's fucking hard being a dad, and sometimes I wonder why I'm the one who ended up with him when I'm sure someone else could be doing a better job. But after everything, if I had to do it all over again, I wouldn't change a thing."

"You can't mean that," I said.

"Finding Ben on my doorstep was a shock. But I love him to death. And if you do this with Ava...it will be the two of you. You and Ava will be doing it together, and you can't give a kid anything more than that. It's what they deserve. And it's what you deserve."

"Don't talk to me about what I deserve," I said.

I couldn't do this. Ava deserved a man who would be there for her no matter what, someone who wasn't so fucking scared of the future. She deserved a man who would be a father her baby could look up to, and that wasn't me. I wasn't a good role model. I drank, I gambled, I slept around...was that the sort of man a kid could look up to?

"She'll find someone else," I said in a hoarse voice. "Someone who will be there for her."

"Are you shitting me?" Gunner asked. "The whole reason you dumped her is because you thought she found someone else."

He was right, but there was some kind of method in my madness. Wasn't there?

She could find a man who would be there for her, someone who would dote on her and be there for the baby and do it all right from the start. Someone who would love her and cherish her.

The more I thought about what would be the right thing—that she had a good man by her side—the more pissed off I got. Just thinking about her having another man upset me. Because I wanted her. I wanted her laughter in my house. I wanted her sharp mind to challenge me. I wanted to be there to celebrate her ups and be there to help her through her downs. The thought of someone else doing that just made me downright jealous.

And the baby...that was *my* kid.

"Damn it," I cursed.

"What now?" Aaron asked.

I shook my head. "I want her in my life."

"Then have her," Gunner said. "She's still your wife, you know."

"I'm so scared I'll fuck it all up," I admitted.

"The only way you can fuck it up," Aaron said. "Is by not caring, not helping, not being there for her. The only way you can fail at being a good husband is—"

"By doing what I'm doing now," I said.

It hit me like a bus. I was fucking it up. The only reason I would lose her was if I didn't fight for her. I couldn't afford to lose her.

Somewhere between showing my dad I could do what I wanted, and trying to keep the pieces of my heart together, I fell head over heels in love with Ava. The thought of losing her had been so terrifying since I'd pushed her away.

But that was exactly what had happened—I'd lost her. Because of *me*.

"I have to go," I said.

"You do that."

"I have to get her back." I pulled out my wallet to pay for our drinks.

"Just go," Gunner said. "We've got this."

I ran out of the bar and to my car. I had to go see Ava. I had to tell her that I'd been wrong, that I should never have let her go. I had to apologize and make it up to her, because I wanted this. I'd been hiding from the fact that she was the one I wanted, that marriage and family with her were like a dream come true when nothing else had made sense.

I had to tell her I loved her.

19

Ava

"You have to open it," Paige said.

I sat on my mom's couch with an envelope in my hands. My fingers trembled, and I was too damn scared to open it.

"I can't," I said.

"I'll do it for you," Paige offered.

"You're going to be fine, honey," Mom said. "Whichever way this goes."

My mom had been amazing the last couple of days. After my dad had died, she'd given up and slowly withered away, and it had taken a lot of time to try to coax her back into wanting to live.

But she looked good now. Her eyes were bright. She was collected and put-together again. She washed her hair often, did her makeup, got up, and got dressed in the morning.

I knew it was because of the money—without all the debt weighing so heavily on us, she was okay again, and she would survive losing my dad.

Instead, I was the one who needed the constant emotional support. I was pregnant, about to be divorced, and I had no idea which way to go with my life now that I was going to be a mother. I didn't even know if I would be a lawyer.

At least my mom was there for me. And Paige. I had a support network, and that was everything. I hadn't wanted to tell my mom how things had turned out with Noah. I hadn't wanted to tell her that I'd gotten married for money. But after everything had fallen apart, I'd had to tell her, and she was so much more forgiving than I'd thought she'd be.

She'd always been in my corner.

"Why did the results come so soon?" I asked.

Usually, the bar exam results arrived one to three months after writing the exam. It had come in the mail so fast, I was suspicious.

"It has to mean I've failed, right?"

"I don't see how it can mean that," Mom said. "You just have to open it and see."

I shook my head. If I didn't open it, I could dare to dream a little longer.

"Look, whether you open it or not won't change what the actual results are," Paige said. "You're either still a paralegal, or you're a lawyer. The only difference is that you don't know exactly what you are right now. Don't you want to find out?"

I nodded. Of course, I wanted to find out. But at the same time, I was terrified.

"Okay, fine," I said and ripped open the envelope. It was time to put this business behind me so that I knew how to move forward.

I opened the results and scanned it. My heart thundered in my chest as my blood rushed to my ears.

I read over the results and froze.

"Well?" Paige asked, excited.

"Oh, my God," I breathed.

"What does it say?" Mom asked, as excited as Paige.

I shook my head, my eyes stinging with tears.

"Here," Paige said, grabbing it. "I can't take it anymore." She looked at the paper before she squealed. "You did it! Ava, you passed!"

"Barely," I said. "My marks are *so* low."

"But it's a pass," Paige said. "And that means you're a lawyer!"

She grabbed me and hugged me. My mom jumped up and did the same. Paige did a little victory dance on my behalf.

"Oh, honey, I'm so proud of you," Mom said.

I sat on the couch in a daze. I hadn't expected this. I'd convinced myself that I would fail, that this was the end of my dream of becoming a lawyer. Somehow, I'd managed to pass the bar exam.

"Do you know what this means?" Paige asked.

"What?" I asked, struggling to wrap my mind around the facts.

"It means that you're going to get a new job, one that pays more, and you're going to do what you've always wanted to do."

My face slowly broke into a smile as I realized what this meant. I was going to be a lawyer. After working as a paralegal all this time, I was going to get what I wanted.

The moment I thought of it, I thought of Noah. It was because of him I'd taken this exam at all. He'd believed in me and pushed me to try another time. If it hadn't been for him...

This victory was bittersweet. I wished I could share it with him. What would he say if he found out I'd passed? He'd probably tell me he'd known I could do it all along.

My smile faded again.

Everything about being a lawyer was tainted now. I could apply at my offices to be a lawyer, they could hire me. But that would mean I would start working there as a lawyer, and soon I would be a junior associate who worked with one of the seniors, or one of the partners. And that meant working much closer to Noah.

I couldn't do that. It was already bad enough that everything at the office reminded me of him. Even though he hadn't been into the office at the same time I'd been there the past week.

"I'll start sending out applications to work at another firm," I said.

"Are you sure that's what you want to do?" Paige asked.

She took my hand when I nodded, and I looked at her before I looked at my mom.

'This is the perfect time to start over. I want my career to be a happy thing. I don't want it to be overshadowed by the pain of everything that had happened in the last couple of months."

Paige nodded. "I get it. And I think it's a great idea."

"Do you really think it is?" Mom asked. "Don't you think that you should hold on to something where you know you have stability?"

I shook my head. "I think I need to start over. I have a lot of money in savings after I'd put it all away and worked as hard as I did, so I can afford to take the time to start over. And after I have the baby, I think I'm going to need it."

Paige took my hand and squeezed it.

"You're going to be okay," Mom said. "You've always been so smart about things, and you're going to be just fine. You have us, and you have savings, and you have everything you need to be an exceptional mother."

I smiled, trying my best to be happy. Paige and my mom were on my side, so excited about the baby and my future. I just wished I could feel as excited about it as they did. I kept thinking about Noah, and that I had to do this without him.

A lump rose in my throat and I tried to think about something else. The last thing I wanted was to cry in front of Paige and my mom when they were both so happy for me.

"I have to go," I finally said. I wanted to get away.

"Where?"

"I have a few things to do at the office," I said.

"On a Saturday?"

I nodded. Work never slept. And neither did I these days. It would have been better if I did—as soon as the baby came, I probably wouldn't have a lot of sleep either. But right now, too much was going on for me to be able to relax and just fall asleep.

Whenever I closed my eyes, I saw his face.

I stood, hugged my mom and Paige, and left the house. I drove to the office, although I didn't know what I would do there. I'd taken care of everything so I could take the weekend off for a change.

The office was empty when I got there. I was relieved—I struggled to keep up a happy face and pretend like nothing was wrong in front of everyone I worked with. Belinda kept asking me if I was okay, which meant that I didn't have a great poker face. And if I told her what was wrong, I had to tell her what had happened between me and Noah, and then the news would be out that we'd gotten married.

Soon, we would be divorced, and then it wouldn't matter anymore.

I sat down behind my desk, powered up my laptop, and stared at the screen. Six months ago, Noah had asked me to marry him. Right here in my office.

I scrubbed my hands down my face. This was exactly why I had to find a new job, so I could get away from the twisted memories that filled this place.

My phone rang, and I dug for it in my bag. My heart suddenly beat in my throat. What if it was Noah? Would he call me? God, I hoped so.

When I pulled out my phone, it was Kyle's number on my caller ID. I rolled my eyes and considered ignoring the call, but I changed my mind. I picked up the phone and held it against my ear.

"Why are you calling me?" I asked.

"Oh, you answered. I thought you were going to just let it roll over to voicemail and your mailbox is full…"

"You're the one who filled it," I pointed out.

"I know, I'm sorry. I just wanted to talk to you. I know you asked me to leave you alone, and this doesn't exactly qualify—"

"It really doesn't.

He sighed deeply. "Look, Ava, I know you're married and everything, but I really just want to see you again. We can be friends, right?"

"Kyle, listen to me," I said. I had to end his misery once and for all. "It's not going to happen. We can't be friends—people who break up can't be friends. It rarely actually works. You need to forget about me, forget about whatever we had, and find someone new. I have." Saying it hurt. I'd found someone alright…and I'd lost him again.

"Can't we just—"

"No, Kyle. We can't. Don't call me again. If you don't respect my wishes, I'm going to have to take legal action."

"What?" he said. "You'd do that?"

"I am in a law career. I know what I'm doing."

"Okay," Kyle said, and he sounded so dejected I imagined he wanted to cry. I could cry, too. But not for the same reasons. "I really hope you're happy, Ava."

"You too," I said.

I ended the call before he could say anything else, and let out a shuddering breath. He hoped I was happy.

God, I hoped I would be happy one day, too. Even though I was on the brink of a divorce, and pregnant with a baby I had no idea how I was going to raise alone. A lump rose in my throat, my eyes stung with tears, and this time I didn't do anything to hold it back. I let the tears flow, and they rolled over my cheeks and fell onto my desk.

Damn it! When Noah had bailed me out by making all those payments for me, I'd thought that everything was taken care of, and my life would finally go in the direction I needed it to go.

Now, it looked like I was getting everything I wanted...but I wasn't happy.

Not even close.

I'd lost Noah, and now it felt like rather than coming together, everything was falling apart.

20

Noah

I knocked on the door of the old Victorian house and stepped back, waiting for the door to open. I drummed my fingers against my thigh, nervous as fuck.

When the door opened, it was an older woman who looked a lot like Ava.

"Hi," I said. "Mrs. Brooks?"

"Yes?"

A blonde woman appeared next to her, and I suddenly recognized her.

"Paige," I said. "What are you doing here?"

"I think I should be asking you the same question," Paige said and folded her arms over her chest.

"Is this him?" Mrs. Brooks asked.

"Yeah, this is him," she said it like it was a bad thing.

"Is Ava here?" I asked.

"Yeah, well, she isn't with you, is she?" Paige said sarcastically.

I shook my head. "Look, I get that you're pissed at me. And you have every reason to be. I just need to talk to her."

"Don't you think you've done enough?"

"Let me talk to her. Let me explain myself." Paige stepped forward and shut the door behind her so that it was just the two of us. Mrs. Brooks allowed it, stepping back.

"I don't know what you're trying to do coming here, but you've hurt her. A lot. I get that you guys didn't plan this thing to be long-term, but she's pregnant now, and it's your baby, and you can't just wish that away like you're doing with everything else."

I frowned. "I'm not wishing her away. You don't get it. I love her."

Paige blinked at me.

"That's what I'm here to tell her," I added when she didn't say anything. "I want to tell her that I love her."

Paige narrowed her eyes at me. "You're serious, this time?"

"What do you mean, this time?" I asked. "I never said anything about love before. I married her because we both needed something out of it, and getting married solved a lot of problems. It was never about love. But somewhere in the middle, something changed, and I want to tell her that. I don't want her to have to go through this alone. I want to be there for her. I want to get her back so that we can do it right."

Paige's face crumpled a little. "Are you serious?"

"Yeah," I said. "For the first time in over ten years, I'm dead serious. I want her in my life. Nothing about life without her appeals to me anymore. I want to get her back."

"Well..." Paige said, "...then you're going to have to make a grand gesture."

I chuckled. "A what?"

"You can't have a fairy tale ending without a grand gesture. Everyone knows that."

"What am I supposed to do?" I asked.

Paige thought about it.

"I think I have an idea, but it's going to take a bit of work to pull it off."

"If it gets me Ava, I'll do whatever it takes."

Paige grinned. "Okay, come in." She pushed the door open. "Lavina, this is Noah. Noah, this is your mother-in-law, Lavina."

"Hi," I said awkwardly.

"Noah is going to fight to get Ava back," Paige said matter-of-factly. "And we're going to help him do that."

"I'll make us coffee," Lavina said. "Sit, make yourself at home."

I sat down, and Lavina hurried out of the living room.

"Okay," Paige said, turning to me. "Listen carefully."

21

Ava

"Is this Ava Brooks?" a woman's voice asked over the phone when I answered an unknown number.

"Yes, speaking," I said.

"We received your resume for the job with Newmark and Lewis. You seem like a great candidate for the position, and we want to invite you in for an interview."

"Oh," I said and glanced up through my glass office walls, checking that no one heard me. Taking a call from a potential new job in my office at Solomon, Forger, and Riggs felt like a betrayal. "I'd love to come see you."

"Great. We'd like to see you tomorrow morning at ten."

I winced. "Ten?"

"Is that a problem?"

"No," I said. "I'll make a plan. If you'll send me the address, I'll be there."

"We'll send it through," the woman said, and we ended the call.

Belinda appeared at my door.

"Are you busy?" she asked.

I shook my head. "Not right now. What's up?" I forced a smile, trying to look like nothing was wrong. Because nothing was wrong, right? I'd just scheduled an interview with a new firm during business hours tomorrow.

"Good, I need you to look at these two files for me. It's a big one. Noah is running point on this case, and you're the only paralegal who can handle this. You're free to take it, right?"

I hesitated. "Noah's running point?"

"Yeah," Belinda said and rolled her eyes. "I know he's being a pain in the ass these days, but it's a big one and you really want to stay on this one. Trust me. If you can impress the big guys upstairs, you're in for whatever might follow in your career."

I nodded and felt like a complete traitor. Archie Forger had hired me, and he was the one I was betraying by going to a new firm behind his back. It wasn't his fault that Noah had screwed me over the way he had.

"Let me know what you think when you go over these, okay? And then we'll be meeting tomorrow morning at ten to see where we stand."

"At ten?" I asked, blood draining from my face.

"Yeah, Noah's in court at eleven, so we can't do it any other time. We really need this one—we can't afford to lose this client, and you know how serious Archie is about Noah keeping his track record straight."

My stomach twisted. "Okay."

I had to call back Newmark and Lewis and let them know that I couldn't do ten for the interview. I hoped they had another time slot I could take. How else could I do this?

When Belinda left, I flipped open the files and scanned the case before I picked up my phone and dialed the number I'd gotten the call from.

It just kept ringing.

The rest of the day, I worked on my research, and kept trying Newmark and Lewis. And no matter how many times I tried to call, I didn't get through.

So far, Newmark and Lewis were the only company that had called me back. It had been a couple of days since I'd sent out my resumes, and I'd hoped a lot more would have contacted me by now. But I only had experience as a paralegal, not as a lawyer, and that made life a lot harder with me applying for a new position.

By the time I called it quits to go home, it was nearly midnight, and I felt sick with nerves. Although, these days, I felt sick of everything. Pregnancy was a bitch. I had to think of something to do tomorrow, a way to get out of Noah's case.

Mom was already asleep when I got home, and when I called Paige, her number went straight to voicemail. I didn't leave a message—she would just feel bad that she'd missed the call when I had a meltdown over the phone, and I didn't want to make her feel bad.

I woke up before my alarm, and I couldn't sleep anymore. I took a shower, got dressed, and went into the office. As the time crept closer and closer to ten, I got more and more stressed about the interview. If I didn't arrive, I wouldn't get the job, and I would be stuck here. If I wasn't here, Noah might lose the case, and it would affect his track record, affect his working relationship with his father...

Why was I worried about that? Why, after everything he'd done to me, did I still care about what he thought and what happened to him?

I knew the answer to that. Because I cared about him. I cared about his relationship with his father. Now that I knew him, I didn't see an asshole who went out of his way to make others' lives miserable, a selfish man who only went for what he wanted and didn't care about anyone else. I saw someone who kept fighting to be himself in a world where he was always expected to be someone else. I saw someone who kept running away from a past that still haunted him. And in a lot of ways, I understood him.

It was getting harder and harder to hate him. After what had happened between us, that was pathetic.

But I couldn't help myself.

By ten, I sat in the boardroom, feeling like shit. I was missing the interview because I'd chosen him, even though he wouldn't choose me. That just made me ridiculous. I was a sucker for punishment. I'd known from the start he would be trouble in my life. From that first night we'd slept together, I'd known he would only trample on my heart. And here I was, waiting for him to do it again.

At ten minutes past ten, Belinda walked into the boardroom where I was waiting.

"Here you are," she said.

I frowned. "Where else would I be?"

"Noah's not coming."

"What!?" I cried out.

"Something came up. He asked me to let you know. If you can just leave those files in his office, he'll look at it as soon as he gets a chance, and—"

While Belinda was talking to me, anger had bubbled up inside me until I felt like I was going to boil over.

"What the hell am I still doing here?" I cried out.

"What?" Belinda asked, confused.

"I give up everything for him, and he doesn't care! I keep thinking he's the worst man in the world, but then he does something that redeems himself, and just when I think there's more...he does it again! He shows me he's the worst man in the world!"

"I'm sorry, Ava," Belinda said carefully. "I don't know—"

"I need to go," I said, cutting her off. I pushed past her and ran to my office, grabbing my handbag. I was so late for the interview, I would probably miss it. But I had to try. I couldn't just let it go.

I left the building in a hurry. The elevator felt like it had crawled down the building at a snail's pace. When I got into my car, there were so many cars on the road it could well have been peak hour traffic.

"Come on, come on," I said, banging my hand onto the steering wheel as if it was going to make a difference. My stomach twisted and turned, and panic threatened to choke me. I forced myself to breathe slowly, in through my nose, out through my mouth.

It took me nearly twenty minutes to get across town to an address that should have only taken ten minutes to get there. The non-descript building was in a more rundown part of town, and looked a little shabby.

"I'm here for an interview," I told the woman at the front desk. "It was at ten."

"You're late," she said.

"I know. It's a long story. Is there a chance I can still take it?"

"I'll call up," she said and picked up her phone. I waited while she talked to the person in charge. She drew circles on a notepad while she talked, and she looked downright bored. I glanced around the building while I waited. The whole place looked like it was falling apart. It wasn't very promising. Would they be able to match my salary? Could I be a lawyer here who made a difference?

"You can go up," she said. "Take the staircase, two floors up, first door on your right."

"The stairs?"

"The elevators are out of order right now. We're working on it." She offered me an empty smile.

I nodded and ran toward the stairs.

When I got to the second floor, I was out of breath. I knocked on the door.

When it opened, Noah stood before me.

I blinked at him, confused. I glanced one way down the hallway, and then the other.

"What are you doing here?" I asked.

"Are you here for the interview?"

"What?"

"Come on in," he said.

I shook my head. "I don't understand. What's going on?"

"Just come in and we'll—"

"No," I said, stepping back. "You're supposed to be back at the office. With *me*, working on this super important case that I nearly missed this interview for. But you weren't there. And now you're here, and—"

"Will you just come inside?" Noah asked.

I shook my head. "I can't play this sick game you keep setting up for me."

"It's not a game, Ava."

"I have to go," I said.

"What about your interview?"

I pressed my hands to my head. "Why are you doing this to me? I don't understand what's going on. You seem set on ruining my life. All I want is to start over. You told me you're not interested, and I'm trying my best to get back on my feet, to do this without you. And you're here, when you should be—"

"You chose me," he said, cutting me off.

"What?" I asked, confused.

"You had a choice between an interview that might change your life, and doing something for me after I treated you like shit. And you chose me."

I shook my head. "I don't know what you're saying."

"I love you."

I stared at him. None of this made sense. It was getting more and more bizarre, and I was just getting more confused.

"I fell in love with you, even though I told myself I wouldn't. And now that I'm about to lose you, I realize that I want you in my life. I want you by my side, as my wife. I want the whole thing—the family, the cozy home, raising kids together, date nights...all of it."

"You told me you didn't want to be with me," I said in a small voice.

"Yeah. I know. I was wrong. I was too scared to be with you because Adele hurt me. We were together once upon a time, and she slept with someone else, and instead of just dealing with it, I went on this binge drinking, whoring around phase that did nothing to help me, it just pushed it all away. It took losing you to realize that I want you. I'm a guy. Sometimes I'm slow on the uptake."

I wanted to cry. His speech was incredible, and a lump rose in my throat. This was exactly what I wanted him to say. I didn't know if I could trust it. This was Noah, the man who made me crazy. I loved him so much, it hurt. And then he hurt me so much, I didn't know which way was up anymore.

"I don't know what to say," I said.

Noah sighed. "Just come into the damn room." He grabbed my hand and pulled me into the office that I was directed to for the interview.

The blinds were drawn, and candles had been put on all the surfaces. Rose petals had been scattered on the floor, and soft music played.

"What's this?" I asked.

"This is your interview."

"What?"

"Ava…" Noah said, taking both my hands in his, "…when we got married, you offered me a foot in the door with my father. But without realizing it, you gave me so much more. You turned my house into a home, making it the one place I wanted to be when going home was something I always dreaded. Instead of a partner in crime, I found a companion. And instead of just a woman I married, I found a wife, and now the mother of my child."

"Noah—"

"Let me finish," he said. "In the position I'm offering you, you'll have a man by your side who dotes on you, who gives you what you want and what you need. I'm offering you a loving environment, financial security, and love."

"Love?"

"I told you I love you. I'll say it again. I'll say it as many times as you need. And if you choose to accept this position, I'll say it every day for the rest of our lives together. So, what do you say?"

I didn't know what to say. My eyes stung, but the fear and anger that had been lodged in my chest since the night Noah had kicked me out had melted.

"I love you, too," I said.

"So, you accept the position?" Noah asked.

I nodded.

He got down on one knee.

"What are you doing?" I asked.

Noah pulled out a black box from his blazer pocket and opened it.

"Ava, will you marry me?"

"We're already married," I said as tears rolled down my cheeks.

"I know. I want to stay that way. I want to do the big white wedding, the honeymoon, the kids. I want Thanksgiving and Christmas with the family. I want date nights and a romantic getaway on Valentine's Day. I don't just want to be married to you. I want us to be together as husband and wife, the way it should be. Be my wife, be my love, be my everything, Ava."

The tears rolled freely now, and I nodded. How could I say no to him? He was probably going to drive me crazy. We were going to fight a lot. But he was right. Even though he drove me mad, I would choose him every day.

"I'll marry you," I said.

Noah smiled and took the ring from the box. He slid it onto my finger, and it fit perfectly.

"Paige helped me," Noah said. "It had to be perfect, and who else to ask but your best friend?"

"Paige helped you?" I asked.

Noah grinned. "Looks like I finally got her approval."

He stood and pulled me tightly against him. "I love you, Ava."

"I love you, too."

He kissed me, and the whole world fell away. When he held onto me, nothing else mattered.

"I really want to offer you a job," Noah said when we finally broke the kiss.

"At a seedy building on the wrong side of town?" I asked, smiling.

"No," Noah said with a chuckle. "Although this was the only place I could rent at such short notice to get this whole thing set up. I want to offer you a job with us. Solomon, Forger, and Riggs. As a junior associate."

"Are you serious?" I asked, frowning. "Can you hire me?"

"No," Noah said. "But I don't care so much about making partner just yet. I have a lot more to learn about life. I think my dad had a point when he said I wasn't ready. He'll be the one to officially offer you the job, but I already talked to him about it, and he's on board with it." He pressed his forehead against mine. "So, what do you say? Do you want to work with me, see me every day, be my partner in justice as much as you're my partner in crime?"

"That's so corny," I said with a giggle.

"I know," Noah said with a shrug.

"I'd love to," I answered. "I want to be your everything."

He kissed me again, and I melted into his arms.

This morning, everything had seemed wrong. Now, everything was right.

And it looked like there was going to be a lot of right for a long time.

A whole lifetime with Noah, to be precise.

22

Ava

I couldn't wait to get back to Noah's place. The office he'd rented had been crazy cute and romantic, but it wasn't the type of place I wanted to strip him naked and show him exactly how I felt about the way he proposed and what he'd said to me.

I followed him in my car and parked in the spot he'd allocated to me when I'd moved in. Noah was at my car before I opened my door, and when I got out, he pulled me tightly against him and kissed me.

His tongue slid into my mouth, and I moaned softly. I ran my hands over his washboard abs and his chiseled pecs, scraping my nails over the button up shirt and Noah gasped into my mouth.

"Let's go," he growled and grabbed my ass, grinding himself against me so that I could feel his erection, his need for me. It only echoed my own need.

We walked through the lobby, waving at the doorman on the way through. In the elevator, Noah and I stood side by side, arms brushing together. The tension between us was palpable, the atmosphere electric. But we behaved for the cameras. I wanted all of this behind closed doors. I didn't want the security team privy to what I wanted Noah to do to me next.

As soon as we were in the apartment, Noah grabbed me again and kissed me. He kicked the door shut behind us without ceremony, and we kissed while we stumbled through the living room on our way to the hallway that would lead to his bedroom.

His fingers found the zipper at the back of my pencil skirt, and he pulled it down. I wriggled out of the skirt and stepped out of it when it pooled around my legs, leaving it on the floor along with my kitten heels I'd worn.

I unbuttoned Noah's shirt while he alternated between his tongue in my mouth and his lips on my neck. I stumbled, and Noah wrapped an arm around my waist to stop me from falling. The symbolism wasn't lost on me. He was there for me in ways a man had never been before, and it meant everything.

When we finally reached the room, I was out of my clothes, walking in my underwear. Noah's shirt was missing, and his pants were open, his erection straining against his boxer briefs.

I pulled his pants down, taking his underwear with them, and his cock sprang free, hard and delicious. The tip oozed lust, and I wrapped my fingers around his shaft.

Noah stepped around, kicking off his shoes and his pants as I'd done with my skirt.

I sank to my knees in front of him, and he groaned, pushing his hands into my hair.

"God, yes," he breathed when I sucked his head into my mouth and leaned forward, taking him in as deep as I could. His hands in my hair curled into fists, and he encouraged me to take him deeper, to suck him off faster. I gave him what he wanted, and his grunts and groans were flattering. The feel of his cock in my mouth, the smooth skin over his thick hardness was a turn on and I got wetter and wetter for him, soaking my panties.

I listened to Noah's breathing. We'd been together long enough for me to know when he was getting close, and I pulled back when his breathing came in short, shallow gasps. I glanced up at him. I didn't want him to come in my mouth. I wanted him to come inside of me, to mark me, to claim me as his.

Because I would be his.

Forever.

"You're so fucking incredible, Ava," Noah said in a hoarse voice, and took my hand to help me up. When I stood, he unclasped my bra and dropped it to the floor. His hands cupped my breasts, and he kissed me, slowly and sensually. He massaged me, his fingers working over my breasts in circles, and I moaned.

Noah nudged me toward the bed and we fell onto the mattress together.

While we made out, Noah's hand slid down my body, and he pushed it into my panties. When his fingers found my clit, I gasped at the same time he groaned appreciatively.

"Fuck, you're wet," he said.

"You should be used to that by now."

He grinned. "I don't think I'll ever get used to how you feel. Everything about you is better than I always remember. And my recollections are nothing short of amazing."

I giggled and blushed, hard. He was a charmer—I'd thought so from the start—but I still fell for his words. It was because he meant them. When we'd first met, his words had been geared to getting into my pants, and that was the end of it. It had worked, too. But now, he meant every word he said to me, and knowing that he'd chosen me, that we were together, and he honestly cared and wanted to give his heart to me, the words he spoke had so much more weight to them.

I trailed a finger along his jaw while he rubbed circles around my clit. I nibbled on his bottom lip and moaned into his mouth. His tongue slid over my lips, and he probed my mouth, tasting, exploring.

Noah retrieved his hand only for long enough to work my panties down my hips. I helped him, pushing them down to my knees, and then I scissored my legs to kick them off. I opened my legs for Noah, and he took his time, first slipping one finger in, then two. I cried out as the pleasure blossomed at my core, the introduction to an orgasm that would follow.

Noah alternated between my clit and my entrance. He rubbed circles around the bud until I was so close I couldn't think about anything other than the pending pleasure. When I was close, he pushed his fingers into me, changing the focus, and the orgasm slid away again, only to start building.

I moaned and cried out, frustrated and in ecstasy at the same time.

"Fuck, Noah," I begged. "Please. You're driving me mad."

"Please?" he asked. "What do you want me to do?" He grinned at me. He knew exactly what I needed, but he was holding out on me.

"Please make me come," I begged. I was hungry for a release, and him keeping me on the edge, teasing me, was torture.

Noah pushed his fingers into me again, and I moaned and gasped as he pumped them in and out. He pressed his thumb against my clit, and balanced me between his hand on my pussy and his lips on my mouth.

He pushed me closer to the edge, and then I toppled over, finally getting the release I'd begged for. I cried out as the waves of pleasure crashed down on me. I gasped, and my mouth rounded in a silent O of pure bliss. I curled my body against Noah, and gasped again as the pleasure subsided, breathing harder.

Noah grinned at me. "You have no idea how hot you are when you do that."

I blushed, drained after the wild orgasm.

Noah rolled against me, his erection thick against my side, and he cupped my breast. I lay on his other arm, and he kissed me, his tongue sliding into my mouth. For a while, we lay together, and he kissed me and caressed me, slowly grinding himself against me. The motion was sensual and tender, and I got lost in the feel of him against me, the way he held me as if I was delicate.

Our kissing grew more and more urgent, and Noah's hands became rougher on my breasts, until his hand branded my skin, and his cock was scalding hot against my hip.

He rolled onto me without a word, breaking the kiss but his face was close enough that our breath mingled together.

My thighs fell open for him, and he positioned himself at my entrance. I held my breath, and when he slid into me, I moaned as my body stretched to accommodate his size.

He buried himself deep inside of me, and I trembled around him. We looked at each other. His eyes were impossibly blue, his lips parted, and his breathing was shallow. He ran his hands through my hair and down my cheek before he kissed me.

"I love you, Ava," he said when he broke the kiss.

We were so close, connected, merged together, so that I had no idea where I ended, and he began. And he was everything I didn't know I needed.

"I love you too," I said.

He kissed me again, before he started moving. He slowly pulled out of me and pushed back in. He kept his strokes slow and long, his eyes locked on mine the entire time he slid in and out of me, and I cried out and moaned and gasped as he filled me up.

Noah picked up his pace, moving faster and faster. I moaned and my breathing came in ragged gasps as he pounded into me faster and faster. He bucked his hips, pumping into me, and the feeling of him was amazing.

It didn't take long before another orgasm built at my core, and with Noah steadily bucking his hips, I came undone in no time at all. The pleasure the second time around was even more incredible than the first.

Noah kissed me after I cried out and gasped and moaned.

"You're beautiful," he said. "Get on top of me."

I smiled at him, and he pulled out, shifting so that he lay on his back. I clambered onto him, straddling his hips, and guided his cock to my entrance before I sank down onto him. He groaned and gripped my hips. I shifted and adjusted, and braced my hands on his chest when I moved my hips back and forth. I bucked them harder and harder, sliding him in and out of me.

Noah's lips parted, and he sucked in a breath through gritted teeth. His gaze moved between my eyes, where he looked at me with love and affection, and my breasts, where his face changed to an expression of pure lust.

I rode him harder and harder, and Noah helped me with his hands on my hips, pulling me forward, pushing me back.

My clit rubbed against his pubic bone, and I cried out as the friction pushed me closer to yet another orgasm. I gasped and moaned, my knees rubbing against the sheets, and Noah's gasping and breathing suggested he was getting closer and closer, too.

For a moment, I thought about a condom. We hadn't put one on—it had slipped my mind completely. But I was pregnant, it wouldn't matter now.

The thoughts were strangely freeing. Noah and I were as safe as we could get right now, and whatever came, we were going to face it together.

I didn't think about the rest of it. I shoved the thoughts of our future as a family away to revisit later and focused on the here and now.

A moment later, I collapsed on Noah's chest, an orgasm rocking my body. Noah held onto me and bucked his hips from beneath, and then he buried himself inside of me and orgasmed, too. He bit out grunts and groans as his cock pulsed and jerked, filling me up even more than I already was.

It felt like our orgasms lasted forever, and we rode out the wave of ecstasy together. Noah and I were together, and no matter what happened, we would face it as a team.

When the orgasms finally subsided, I lay on his chest for a long time. I listened to his heartbeat slowing, his breathing even out. He stroked my back in circles.

"I could stay here forever," I said.

"Move back in with me."

"Right now?"

"Yeah," Noah said. "Stay tonight. We'll pick up your stuff in the morning, and we'll take care of the rest later."

I nodded. "Okay."

"Yeah?"

"Yeah," I said with a grin. "But I have one condition."

"What's that?" he asked.

"I don't want my old room back. I prefer this one."

When Noah spoke, I could hear the smile in his voice.

"That's a pity, because this is my room."

"I guess we'll just have to share, then." I lifted my head and looked up at him. He grinned at me before he kissed me.

"Oh, I have news," I said.

"What?"

"I passed the bar."

"I know, why do you think I offered you the junior associate position? Paige clued me in."

"Oh, right." I blushed.

Noah laughed, the sound of pure happiness rumbling through his chest as it echoed in my bones, too.

23

Noah

"Hey, Dad," I said when we parked my car and I led Ava into my childhood home.

Dad waited for us in the foyer.

"Noah," he said with a curt nod. When he saw Ava, his face split into a smile. "And Ava. Welcome to our home." He liked her, I could tell. My dad was always so serious and grumpy, never buckling or bending for anyone—especially me. But for the past couple of weeks, since Ava and I had decided we were going to do this for real, my dad lit up when he saw her.

I had a sneaky suspicion that despite how upset he'd been with my antics of getting married behind his back, he approved of Ava.

She felt more and more at home with my family, too. I'd worried that after the first meeting, where I'd left because my ex had been there, none of them had a good impression of each other. The good thing about first impressions was the fact that if they were bad to start off with, things could only get better from there.

And they'd gotten better in ways that I'd never been able to imagine.

"Your mother is in the kitchen with your sister," Dad said.

I nodded, and we walked through the house, finding my mom and sister in the state-of-the-art kitchen. Mom arranged flowers in a vase while Celine sat on the counter, kicking her legs like a child.

"Oh, good, you're here!" Celine cried out and hopped off the counter. She came to Ava and hugged her. "How are you? And how is my favorite nephew doing?" She put her hand on Ava's belly. Ava wore a loose top that hid her small baby bump. She was starting to show, but not very much yet.

"We're both fine," Ava giggled.

I watched my sister and shook my head. She could be a real bitch sometimes, and she hadn't been very nice to Ava when she'd met her at the restaurant. We'd both been raised by a family where money was a priority above being warm to people, so I guess it was understandable.

When Ava and I had come to see my family, telling them the news that we were going to make this work, Celine had still been cold toward Ava. I'd pulled her aside and told her to get her shit straight—Ava was here to stay, and I would defend her no matter what. Celine had cleaned up her act since then, and she and Ava seemed to get along just fine, now.

I kissed my mom on the cheek, and she hugged Ava, too. It made me happy to know that Ava fit into my family the way she did.

"What can I do to help?" Ava asked.

"You can help me make a salad," Celine suggested. "Mom wants us to do it instead of just getting a caterer like she always does and now this place has turned into a sweatshop."

"It's not the end of the world, Celine," Mom scolded.

Ava giggled while Celine rolled her eyes, and the two of them got started.

"Noah?" Dad asked from the kitchen door. "Can I talk to you?"

I frowned and nodded. My dad gestured for me to follow him, and we walked through the house to his home office. This route from the kitchen to the office was one I knew all too well—I'd walked it a thousand times before whenever my dad scolded me. I braced myself for whatever would come. It couldn't be so bad. Nothing seemed so bad now that I had Ava by my side. Together, we could get through anything.

Dad gestured to an armchair that faced the desk and shut the door before he walked around, sitting in his own chair.

"Let me get straight to the point—there's no use beating about the bush," Dad said. "I want to talk to you about your career."

I nodded. The last couple of months I'd been married to Ava, I'd done what I'd needed to do to get my cases and win them, but it had been begrudgingly. I'd done what my dad asked, and he still hadn't made me a partner. Now that I had Ava, I realized what was important.

"I worked hard these past couple of months," I said. "I signed a few clients, and I won all my cases and—"

"I know," Dad said. "I've been checking up on you and you're doing great as a senior associate."

"And I'm okay being one for a while, still," I said.

"Are you?" Dad asked, and he frowned, looking confused.

I nodded. "Yeah, I don't think it's such a big deal anymore. Career isn't everything. I mean, I would love to become a partner. But there's still time, right? I'm good where I am now, I can help people, and that's really what matters."

My dad narrowed his eyes at me.

"What?" I asked when the silence stretched out between us, and he still had that suspicious look on his face.

"Where's Noah, and what did you do with him?" Dad asked.

I burst out laughing. "Don't get me wrong, I want to make partner. Badly. But I just know that it's not everything, you know? I mean, I'll get there in time. I have Ava to focus on, and the baby...it's enough."

My dad smiled at me and sniffed.

"Well, that's what I want to talk about," he said. "I haven't made it official yet, but we've been talking at the office and we're going to make you partner."

I blinked at my dad. "What?"

"You heard me. We're going to announce it this week, and it will be official before the weekend. I wanted to give you a heads up so you walk into the celebrations in the office with your eyes open."

I stared at my dad. "Why now?"

"Because you did what I asked, and it's only fair."

I shook my head. "That's not why I went after Ava to get her back. It wasn't some loophole or a way to trick the system this time."

Dad nodded. "I know. And that's exactly why you're getting what you wanted all along. You chose to be with Ava because not only was it the right thing to do, it was what you wanted. More than being a partner. I just wanted you to understand that there's more to life than career and image and what the whole world thinks about you."

I nodded. "I think I get it, now. It took a while—I'm slow on the uptake, apparently."

Dad laughed. "Us Forger men can be fucking headstrong."

"You're telling me," I said.

Dad and I laughed together, and I shook my head. Partner? I couldn't believe it. After all this time, just as I'd realized what was really important, I'd gotten everything I'd wanted all along.

It was all thanks to Ava, though. Without her, I wouldn't have gotten to this point. I wouldn't have realized what mattered, and I would have gone on fucking around and drinking, screwing up my image and dragging the company name through the mud.

After ten years of feeling stuck, feeling like I was untethered and wandering, I'd finally figured out what really mattered.

I'd learned where I belonged.

Ava was my home.

Dad and I stood. I held out my hand, and when my dad took it, I shook his hand.

"Thanks, Dad," I said.

"You only have yourself to thank," Dad said. "You did this."

I nodded. "But you stuck through it with me even though I was a pain in the ass and it means a lot to me."

Dad chuckled. "Just remember this for when your children come because they'll drive you up the wall and make you crazy long before you feel like you're reaping the fruits of your labor."

I laughed. I knew this was going to be a challenging time. We were expecting a son, and if he was anything like the Forgers in our family, he would be a handful just like I was.

But I was ready for it. I had Ava by my side, and my parents at my back, and come what may, we were going to figure this out.

Together.

Epilogue — Ava

Sixteen Months Later

I stood in front of the full-length mirror. A long sheet covered it.

"Ready?" Paige asked.

I took a deep breath and nodded. Paige and Celine glanced at each other, a twinkle in their eyes, before Paige dropped the sheet.

I stared at myself in the mirror.

The white wedding dress had been custom-made especially for me, and it was spectacular. It was a simple strapless dress with a wide skirt, but it was embellished with diamonds all around the bodice and onto the skirt. It looked like I'd been sprinkled with glitter and stars.

My hair was pinned up and back in an elegant updo, and my make-up was perfect.

"Oh, sweetheart," my mom breathed behind me. She had little Warner on her hip, and when she saw me, her eyes misted up. "You're beautiful."

Warner giggled and put one of his chubby fists in his mouth, and I laughed and pinched my baby boy's cheeks. He was ten months old, already strong enough to pull up to standing, although he wasn't taking any steps, yet. He had his dad's piercing blue eyes and my dark hair, and he was adorable.

I didn't know I could love someone as much as I loved Warner. I loved Noah with all my heart, but the love I had for my baby boy was different—so much deeper than anything I'd felt before.

"You look great," Paige said, hugging me. "I can't believe you've come this far! And I can't believe how much you spent on this wedding, either." She laughed.

"She's a Forger," Celine said with a shrug. "We take the term 'all or nothing' very literally."

Paige rolled her eyes. "I don't even want to think about you and all your money."

Celine grinned. "Don't pout, I like the fact that you have so much freedom and no expectations. Every position has a good and a bad side, right?"

Paige wanted to say something, but I put my hand on her arm.

"Let's get a wedding done, guys, let's not fight."

Paige and Celine didn't get along very well. They were from different walks of life and Celine could be a pain in the ass if she wanted to. My sister-in-law was used to getting her way and for the whole world to worship at her feet, and Paige wasn't having any of it. She didn't look up to anyone who didn't deserve it, and it caused the two to butt heads often.

Most of the time, it didn't matter that they didn't get along. Paige would always be my best friend and Celine would always be a sister to me.

It was only now that they were both bridesmaids that things were sticky. Celine had wanted to be the maid of honor, but Paige was my best friend, my ride-or-die.

"Let's go," Paige agreed.

"I'll see you in there," Mom said and kissed me on the cheek. I blew raspberries in Warner's neck until he squealed and giggled—since he'd started smiling, I couldn't get enough of his giggles.

The three of us walked down the hotel hallway toward the elevator. My in-laws had booked out the entire hotel for the wedding of the century.

When we arrived at the doors to the ceremony room, the other two girls—Noah's cousins—waited for us. They gushed over the dress and we took a few quick selfies before we lined up. The music started, and the two cousins walked in first, one following the other before Celine went next.

"Are you ready for this?" Paige asked when it was almost her turn.

"Readier than I've ever been," I said with a smile.

"Good answer. Because you can't exactly change your mind, you've been married for two years."

I giggled. Today was our two-year anniversary. We'd thought it would be poetic to do the big wedding—the one I'd said I didn't want if it wasn't real—today.

"I wouldn't change it for the world," I said with a smile.

Paige looked emotional when she squeezed my hand.

"I'm so happy for you."

"It's your turn," I said, and Paige straightened herself out and turned to step into the room to the beat of the music.

I took a deep breath. My dad wasn't here to walk me down the aisle. I wasn't as upset about it as I'd been before. It had taken a long time for me to get to a point where I'd forgiven him for what he'd done to my mom and me.

I could walk myself down the aisle just fine. I was my own person, and everything I'd done had been my own choice. I was with Noah because I loved him. I didn't need anyone to give me away. I knew exactly where I wanted to go, and I was at the helm of my own ship.

When it was my turn, I stepped into the room. Everyone turned to look at me, and I made eye contact with a few people I knew, smiling. A lot of misty eyes stared back at me, and I swallowed down a lump that rose in my own throat, too.

When my eyes fell on Noah, his face filled with affection. His entourage stood in their suits behind him, and they looked as emotional as everyone else—even Aaron, who seemed to be made of stone most of the time.

"You look incredible," he said when I reached him and he flipped back my veil.

"You clean up pretty well yourself," I said with a smile.

He wore a black tuxedo, and he looked edible. Later, I would do exactly that.

We turned to the officiant, and the ceremony started.

When it was time to read our vows, we turned to face each other.

Noah went first.

"When we met, it wasn't under the best circumstances," Noah said. "And when we got married...well, that wasn't, either. Looking back now, I could have done all of that better."

I giggled and laughter rippled through our audience, too.

"But even though I hadn't gone about it in the best way, you are the best thing that's ever happened to me. I love you more than life itself, and you've shown me what it means to live, to love, to dream. So, today I promise you, Ava Forger, that no matter what lies ahead, I will fight for you and our son, I will protect you, and I will do whatever it takes to make sure that this will forever be our happy ending. I am, and always will be, yours."

I blinked away tears and swallowed hard.

"Noah," I said in a cracking voice and swallowed again, taking a deep breath. "Never in my life have I been happier that someone proved me wrong. You proved me wrong about you every step of the way. Whenever I thought I couldn't find a side of you that was kind and tender, you showed me that you had more dimensions, and that first impressions mean nothing. You helped me when I was drowning, you saved me when I thought my world would crash and burn. And just when I thought there wasn't any more to give, you showed me that I was wrong. Again. I promise to keep giving just as you do—to give myself, my time, my effort, and to put it all into being the best mother and wife I can be. I promise to endeavor to deserve your love every day until the end of time. You're everything."

Noah smiled at me, and when the officiant announced that he could kiss the bride, Noah grabbed me and kissed me so hard my toes curled and I blushed.

"You and me, babe," he said with his forehead against mine and our lips close to each other.

"Forever," I answered.

He kissed me one more time before we turned toward our friends and family. They burst into applause, and Noah took my hand. He pressed it against his lips before we walked back down the aisle together, husband and wife, completely in love, and ready to take on the rest of our lives together.

Also By Josie Hart

Conrad Billionaire Brothers Series

Faking It – A Bad Boy Enemies to Lovers Romance

Secret Baby for the Boss – An Off Limits Brother's Best Friend Romance

Single Dad Bosshole – An Age Gap Enemies to Lovers Romance

Crestwood Billionaires Series

Stuck with the Grump – An Age Gap Brother's Best Friend Romance

Cavalier Billionaires Series

Accidental Baby for the Billionaire – An Enemies to Lovers Second
Chance Romance

32561607R00125